Tall Weeds

ISBN: 0-9882-7090-0
ISBN-13: 9780988270909

Tall Weeds

Stephen Huey

Two Dogs Barking Press
twodogsbarkingpress.com
2012

Dedication

I would like to express my thanks to everyone in the village who assisted in one way or another to write this book: to Captain R. D. Williams who was the first to recommend I write a story about my Balkan adventures; to Tyler Marshall, Jim Marshall, and Kathy Knopf for their outstanding editing and suggestions; to Margaret Huey, my other mother and English teacher, who loves my writing but not my spelling; to my friends and colleagues with the Houston Police Department and UNTAES, particularly Mark and Kazumi; to Dawn Mercurio for her beautiful artwork and Linda Johnson for her exceptional photography. Finally, I am especially grateful and lucky to have had the support and encouragement from two wonderful women, my mother Nancy and my wife Mary. Though my mother passed away in 2007, I'm sure she would have purchased a copy (and I'm sure she's smiling). And if it were not for Mary's love, companionship, and patient listening to my reading aloud (which is horrible) this book would have never come to be.

chapter

ONE

Vukovar, Yugoslavia: November 1944

Drug Stari must die. They made it sound easy. Dying was easy; getting there was the problem.

From his window, Jakcic Radovan saw only clean, crisp snow-covered fields. The tall, thin Serb ran his gaze along the white landscape, then up to silver clouds that raced ahead of late November's moon.

A cord that hung from the ceiling held a single exposed light bulb, which provided the only illumination inside the Spartan one-room farmhouse. This was the sum of his world. With no wife, no children, and no other living family members, the war had taken all he had; now he wanted something back.

Radovan pulled the heavy curtains shut, filled a shot-glass with Rakija, and downed it. *I could turn back; the fools have already paid me. And what are the Nazis going to do, invade my country? They've already done that and they're getting their butts kicked for it.* Yugoslavia wasn't being crushed as the German High Command, OKW, had planned. The damn Slavs under General Josip Tito, *Drug Stari*, were resisting and winning. What was supposed to have been a rout taking only a few weeks had turned into a slog with no end in sight. Men and materials were being sucked into the Balkan nightmare at an alarming rate, and the OKW needed to end the fight as soon as possible. So, when Radovan, a trusted member of Tito's inner circle, turned up as a willing assassin ready to cut off the head of the Yugoslavian Army, the Nazis thought their prayers had been answered. To be sure, Jakcic Radovan and the Nazi High Command were in agreement; *Drug Stari* must die, but their reasons were very different.

After opening a heavy lock on a wooden cabinet, the Serbian turncoat removed several books that concealed a small radio transmitter. He placed it on the table and connected the antenna wire. Diligently, he plugged the power cord into a receptacle holding the solitary light bulb. He flipped the switch on the radio and turned off the light, leaving him in darkness.

As the radio tubes warmed, Radovan's face was washed with the green glow of the instrument. He lit a cigarette, put on the earphones, and tuned in the radio receiver. From his pocket-watch he marked the time, 10:29.

When the second hand on the watch face hit twelve, his broadcast began:

"*Der Schlaf des winters bald beendet.*"

High above, a DFS 230 Nazi transport glider sailed silently through broken clouds. Inside, the burly German jumpmaster stood at the door of the craft and pressed the radio headset against his ear:

"*Der Schlaf des winters bald beendet.*"

He waited for it again.

"*Der Schlaf des winters bald beendet.*"

It was the signal.

Sliding open the portside door, the frozen punch from November's icy wind had little effect on the veteran paratrooper. Holding to the sides of the door, he leaned out and inspected the drop-zone below. *All was going as planned*, he thought.

After pulling himself back inside, the sergeant turned and faced six elite German SS Paratroopers, dressed in their winter whites, watching his every move. He signaled and the soldiers stood in unison. He gave another hand gesture and mechanically they shuffled to the door. Stopping the lead man for a moment, the Nazi jumpmaster checked his watch. Then, on his mark, the sergeant slapped the lead man's back who leaped into the night followed by the other five. Watching from his high perch, the jumpmaster saw all six chutes deploy. He shut the glider's portside door and the paratroopers floated quietly down into the white world below.

***

A shovel spade hit the frozen ground, breaking the silent, bitter air. Radovan's frosty breath-cloud mixed with moonbeams that streamed through the holes in the roof of his shabby barn. After he finished the dig, he wrapped the radio in a burlap sack, placed it into the hole, and covered it with cold earth. His destiny was fixed.

Loud talk and occasional laughter spilled into the snow-covered streets of the ancient Serbian village. Except for sporadic flickers of light that escaped the heavy restaurant curtains, the village of Vukovar was empty, frozen, and black.

Inside the restaurant, a half-empty Rakija bottle, a tobacco pouch, and some rolling papers were at the center of the table where four old Serbian farmers gathered. Each was dressed for warmth as the flames from the low burning fire offered little heat in the dim, smoke-filled room. Without warning, the solid door swung open and all talk went silent with the sudden commotion.

Three men entered, dressed as the other Serbian farmers, but hard, cold eyes showed they were not as their fellows. Though their arrival was a surprise, none of the three were unfamiliar. It was Gen. Tito, followed closely by two young bodyguards armed with stolen German Gewehr 41 rifles.

One of the protectors was a gaunt youth, Kulas Mihjilo. On the surface this skinny kid appeared to be just another ordinary Serbian farm boy. But no one who knew him thought him ordinary, especially the Germans.

Enemy soldiers called Mihjilo the "White Wolf" and for good reason. In three months, his sniper rifle had claimed forty-five Nazi officers, a kill every two days. Needless to say, German commanders could do the math, and this kept them on edge. The other guard was just as ferocious, a highly skilled killer in his own right, Jakcic Radovan.

Taking a seat, the Yugoslavian General casually constructed a cigarette, all the while looking at the haggard faces of every man in the room. His expression revealed many nights without sleep, but sleeping was for the dead.

"A great opportunity has come our way," Tito stated while turning his gaze to Mihjilo. "Yet, it was almost lost because I was deceived." The general's words came alive with fire. "The Austrian Corporal faces his army West because he does not fear Yugoslavia. To him we are beaten, crushed, finished, making it so much the better for us to strike, now! But the Germans have been sent a warning, detailing our plans."

The barrel of a Lugar Po8 pistol planted itself behind the left ear of Kulas Mihjilo. "You fool," said Radovan. With his free hand, he took Mihjilo's weapon, tossed it to one of the other men, and pushed the unsuspecting White Wolf into a chair. Saying nothing, the thin Serb kept his eyes locked upon his accuser. A weird showmanship came over Radovan during the immediate inquisition. He started using his pistol like a wand to conjure up an absurd story of Mihjilo's betrayal. It was a carnival of lies and, like all freak shows, it ended badly.

"We trusted you with our future and this is what you do! To us, your brothers, your country." Radovan spit on Mihjilo. "Ustashe pig! Where's the book holding our treasure? You were told to bring it. You can't keep it for yourself and your German masters." As the false threat built steam inside, the actual threat began to reveal itself outside.

Muffled sounds of boots that broke glazed snow announced the arrival of the German paratroopers into Vukovar. Quietly and quickly, the squad leader moved his soldiers from one building to the next until they reached their objective, the restaurant. Here, the leader split his force. He and two others took positions in the front while the rest of the soldiers went to the rear of the building. *The trap was set*, he thought.

Inside the restaurant, Radovan held a small, black leather-covered manuscript, with an imprint of a three-headed wolf on it. Known simply as "The Book," the information inside was anything but.

Since the time of Rome, and the rise and fall of all the empires thereafter, there had been many kings in the Balkans. This little handbook was their legacy. Within its coded pages lay the location of Byzantine jewels predating the crusades, Turkish gold spread by the invaders, and seventeenth century Habsburg diamonds, an extraordinary treasure passed from one conqueror's hands to the next. Now Gen. Tito used it to support the fight and unite the people. In sum, it was the fate of a nation.

"Who would believe the future of Yugoslavia? Perhaps the war rests in these pages. The wealth of centuries locked inside this little book." Radovan placed his face just inches from Mihjilo. "And you were going to give it away."

Outside, the German squad leader signaled and two paratroopers rose from their positions. They ran across the street toward the restaurant. At that instant a strong hand reached over the top of the Nazi leader's helmet from behind and snapped his head backward. For the second of life left to him, he was eye to eye with a Yugoslav then his throat was slit; silent, quick, lethal.

Next, machine gun fire erupted in front of the restaurant and caught the two Germans in crossfire, cutting them down. Shots rang out from behind the building as well.

A single SS paratrooper survived the initial assault and raced from the back. A Balkan soldier followed closely, stopped, raised his weapon, and fired. Striking his target in the head, the elite SS trooper tumbled dead into the snow. Much to Nazi Germany's displeasure, occupied Yugoslavia wasn't France. The Yugoslavs fought back, always.

Everyone was on the floor inside the restaurant, everyone except Tito, Radovan, and Mihjilo. With the book firmly in his hand, Radovan's pistol was now on *Drug Stari* as well. As the turncoat made his way to the door, he motioned Mihjilo to stand next to the Partisan leader. *An efficient execution; the Nazis will be impressed.*

"You and your Partisans; the West hates you. And the Russians, they only want to rule you. Yet, you continue to fight and waste a fortune. The wealth of the Hapsburgs, the Turks; you hide it in the mountains of Sarajevo, Why?" Jakcic Radovan extended the Luger. "It makes no difference now."

Stephen Huey

From around the corner of the door, the working-end of a MP 34 machine gun came to rest in Radovan's back. "You're right," said Tito, taking a seat. "It makes no difference now. Take the book and his weapons. Come, Mihjilo; sit, my friend." As the general poured himself and the White Wolf drinks, two Yugoslav soldiers entered the room, kept aim at Radovan, and did as instructed. "I thought your loyalty beyond question, Jakcic, but I was told differently. So, I tested you," Tito explained. Another soldier entered with the burlap bag containing the radio the apostate had buried.

With every man's hand against him, Radovan's intrigue was finished. But begging for his life didn't occur to him, nor would it. He took a seat opposite of the Yugoslav leader, rolled himself a cigarette, and reviewed the situation, coolly.

"If the Allies win, they'll next turn on you. None of them care for your dream of Yugoslavia. They only like us because we kill Nazis. Once that's finished, so are we." He then leaned forward and made the last play. "But this doesn't have to be. We can share this wealth."

In silence, all eyes fixed on the traitor. After looking from one person to the next, Radovan recognized his greed was his alone. Taking a pull from his cigarette, he exhaled the smoke slowly. His fate was at the station, and he knew it. Now it was time for him to get onboard. Rising to his feet, he snapped his heels, threw back his shoulders, and awaited his verdict.

A single shot rang out.

chapter

TWO

Vukovar, UN Transitional Area: November 1999

Fifty-five years later, the restaurant now served as a police station for the United Nations Transitional Administration Eastern Slavonia, UNTAES, a truly peculiar organization and territory.

UNTAES came to be after a three-month slaughter in the former Yugoslavia reached its apex in an eighty-four hour free-for-all in August 1995. Initiated by the Croatian Armed Forces, it pitted Croatians and Bosnians against Serbs, Bosnian Serbs, Croatian Serbs, and a few misguided

Bosniaks. It was a bloody mess and the United Nations jumped right into the middle of it.

Wearing blue helmets and waving a peace treaty, UN peacekeepers stopped the war but not the fighting. So, to keep the lid on, more than 400 law enforcement officers from thirty countries were recruited for police work, Balkan style. It was a mess too, but with less blood.

In the station for the night watch were two UN police monitors from the United States. One, Tyler Longvue, was looking out the window at the snow-covered village. On this cold clear night, the full moon coupled with the few working streetlights softened the skeletons of the destroyed buildings.

Longvue, 38, was a good cop with a crooked smile. But people meeting him off-the-job were always surprised to discover that he was a flatfoot. Bookish and thin, the Texan seemed better suited for addressing the board rather than kicking in the door on a drug raid. This was a misconception that had proven handy, but still annoying. His partner was a different story altogether.

Mark Burnwell, the same age as Longvue, sat at a desk working a word puzzle. He was a big man with a bald pate and an endless wit. One look at him and there was no doubt about it, he was *the Heat*. Two weaknesses plagued him though: good-looking women and his many children. Yet, he left six kids and three ex-wives in Utah to volunteer for a year-long mission in a Yugoslavian war zone. He said he needed a break. One needed a sense of humor, especially on this mission.

United Nation's policing was something new for the US contingent. Many of the kinks were still being worked out, like their black uniforms for example. No other police contingent in the mission wore uniforms of this color, and for good reason.

Just a short one war ago, during WWII, a group of fanatical Catholic Nationalist Croatians called Ustashe collaborated with Nazi Germany and adopted their racial purity policies. From 1941 to 1945, this Nazi-backed police force of Ustashe thugs, dressed in all black uniforms, systematically exterminated nearly 300,000 people, the majority being Jews, Romas, and Serbs. Now, in the 1990s, a police force dressed in all black uniforms was back. For the Serbs in the region it wasn't exactly heartwarming.

Lighting a cigarette, Longvue asked, "Do you ever get tired of working crossword puzzles?"

"Nope," replied Burnwell. "Around here it's the only way to get a sense of accomplishment, some satisfaction."

"Hell, take up smoking," said Tyler, taking another pull from his smoke and breaking into a god-awful hack.

"How's that working for you?"

"Another month, Burnwell, and I'm through, through with the Croatians, the Serbians, and you."

"What about the Muslims, Stickman? Nobody pays much attention to them, and that's going to become a big problem someday; but not your problem because you're on the way home. And this circus will just keep going and going and going."

"Look, fatboy, if you think this peacekeeping gig is a failure, why did you push so damn hard to extend for another year?"

"I never said it wasn't going to work. But, Tyler, you can't slap a Band-aid on a decapitation and expect it to heal after one tour of duty. It's going to take a long time."

"Sure, about a generation, but Uncle Sam ain't going to pay for that long. Besides, this part of the world is a tough sell. Most folks back home have never heard of it and even fewer can find it on a map."

"Yeah, I remember when the people at the UN called and said I was going to Slavonia. I said, 'No, there must be some mistake. I volunteered for Yugoslavia.' There was silence for a moment, then the lady said, 'Mr. Burnwell, that is Yugoslavia.'" With a half grin, the big Mormon continued. "Yugoslavia. The Cold War ended, they kicked out the Russians, and what did they do to celebrate? Declared war and carved the joint up in a slaughterhouse."

"These people can't live together, Mark; they hate each other."

"They've always hated each other. But they lived together under the Turks, then the Hapsburgs, then Tito, so why can't they do it now?"

Neither had an answer nor did any other living soul for that matter. Longvue turned his attention back outside, and Burnwell returned to his puzzle.

Vukovar, where the UN police station was located, had served as a large Serb stronghold since the war ended. As part of the deal to stop the fighting, the job of UNTAES was to peacefully hand over the city and a substantial chunk of the surrounding real estate to the Croatians. Needless to say, the Serbs were unhappy because the Croats were forcing them out. Additionally, where it was the Serbs were supposed to go was anybody's guess. And if kicking them out wasn't bad enough, consider how it was being done and by whom. Recall the black uniforms mentioned above.

"Yesterday, I was thinking about when I arrived here last summer," said Burnwell. "The first thing that struck me was the grass. Everywhere I looked, the lawns, the fields, they were out of control, uncut, packed full of tall weeds. I thought, these things need to be mowed and cleaned up; you know, give the neighborhoods a sense of order. But you can't do that. The weeds grow tall because the fields are full of mines. From the outside, the Balkans are beautiful, but get in the door and you find it's a train wreck of a country, wrapped in a mystery, and dripping with hate."

Across the street, the doors of the war-blistered church opened and guests streamed out to form lines on either side. All were people from the village except for two extraordinary exceptions that caught Longvue's attention; one was Kulas Mihjilo, now 77, and the other was Kazuko Nakamura.

A deep red muffler and a shock of white hair accented Mihjilo's dark gray suit and long black winter coat. But it wasn't the clothes that made the man. There was something more, *gravitas*.

Kazuko Nakamura, a smart young human rights officer and a "true believer" in her efforts, was next to Mihjilo, dressed in typical UN garb: khaki, khaki, and more khaki. A janitor's uniform had more panache.

"Well, solve this mystery, Sherlock. Why is Kazuko attending the wedding across the street?"

"No way." Burnwell scrambled to his feet and joined Longvue at the window. "Who's that old guy with her?"

"That, my corpulent friend, is the one and only Justice Kulas Mihjilo."

"Whoa! If the boys at HQ knew he was out just standing in the open, oh man, they'd need life support."

"Ah, the boys at HQ have a pork chop tied to their crank."

"What the hell does that mean, Tyler?"

"It means they're always scared of getting bit."

"Well, they should be. This Mihjilo guy is some kind of weird Serbian mix of George Washington and Bill Gates."

The statement caught Longvue by surprise. Only a few days ago, he was told about the fortune and the book, specifically, in strict confidence. Now, it seemed like he was the last one in on the secret. "What do you know about the treasure?"

"It's the word on the street," said Burnwell as he gathered his hat and coat and made his way to the door. "Stickman, everyone knows that old man has this book that'll lead you to a ton of money."

Longvue picked up his coat as well. "And you believe the story?"

"Of course; I'm Mormon. I believe anything that's fantastic."

It was a noisy, joyous, raucous celebration, like all Serbian weddings in the village. In the courtyard of the small Orthodox Church, all were talking, laughing, and waiting anxiously for the bride and groom to make their way from inside. There was an old Serb granddad in the crowd playing a ukulele and croaking some prehistoric folk song. Another codger joined him, but neither played the same tune. And nothing whipped up the excitement of a wedding crowd more than celebratory AK-47 fire, which was being generously provided by a group of young men. Yes, the rounds will return to earth, but an old Serbian proverb holds these slugs will only find their enemies.

Mihjilo was busy shaking what seemed to be a never-ending stream of hands. Burnwell and Longvue joined Nakamura in the reception line just as the crowd animation jumped. Out burst the married couple, loud went the cheering crowd, and up flew the congratulatory bullets.

"I thought you two were up north attending a meeting," shouted Tyler.

Even though he was next to her, Nakamura could barely hear. "We were," she replied just as loudly. "But the Justice suddenly announced he was leaving for a wedding. He invited me, so, love is a wonderful thing."

Music, booze, and gunfire. Face it, the Serbs knew how to celebrate. And just for a moment, the appalling bleakness of the combat-ravaged village disappeared, but only for a moment.

A gray, 1994 Mercedes S-Class Coupe arrived; the driver exited and opened the rear door for the married couple. The car was a gift from Justice Mihjilo and a great surprise for the bride and groom.

The Justice was having a magnificent time. All the men wanted to pat him on the back or shake his hand, and all the women, both young and old, wanted to kiss him.

Everyone knew the White Wolf, and everyone loved him; well, almost everyone.

An old disheveled Croatian man fixed a flat gaze on Mihjilo. Though clearly a villager, the elderly Croat wasn't part of the celebration. Purposefully, he made his way through the crowd toward the celebrated Serbian Judge. As the bride and groom climbed into the awaiting vehicle, the eyes of the old man and the Justice met. Like a cruel wind coming off the frozen Dinaric Alps, their history was awakened, cold, strong, and merciless. In less than a second, the grizzled chap had a pistol on Mihjilo, but neither man would do more than stand and stare at one another.

"Gun," shouted Tyler, as he leaped at the Croat. Mark also dived and grabbed the elderly man's weapon hand. Leveling the old fellow, the pistol fired on impact, cutting hot lead across the top of Burnwell's leg. "Damn his eyes!" yelled the big man, grasping the wound while he rolled to his side. Meanwhile, Longvue knocked the handgun free and subdued the old man.

As typical in emergency situations, most people were simply stunned. The wedding crowd proved to be ordinary with one notable exception. The young Serbs, armed with their AK-47s, instantly surrounded Mihjilo in protection.

Quick upon this, three black Mercedes 300s stopped near the church. Tinted windows came down, several Uzi SMG machine guns were extended, and automatic gunfire erupted into the wedding party. Dull rapid thuds of bullets ripped into people that sent lifeless bodies to the ground. The rest of the wedding group fled. Like flushing a covey of quail, people shouted, screamed, and ran in all directions to escape death. But Mihjilo stood firm. With a cool presence of mind, he returned fire and maneuvered directions to his young comrades, effectively engaging the attackers. This kind of courage was contagious, as the White Wolf well knew.

Moving in a fast low crawl, Burnwell reached the other side of a nearby stone wall. Longvue let loose of the old Croat, but took his pistol and quickly dashed to Nakamura. Taking her by the arm, he pushed her inside the gray Mercedes along with the wedding couple. But turning to get Mihjilo twisted into an episode from the Twilight Zone.

This was a whole hog firefight, but it didn't faze Mihjilo a jot. Everyone else had run off or taken cover, but not the White Wolf. He was up walking around fearlessly, shouting encouragement to all his boys. There was only one way to get that old warhorse out of there, and Longvue knew he couldn't do it on his belly.

Though the air was heavy with deadly flying ordinance, when Longvue reached Justice Mihjilo, they stood there and discussed leaving with less urgency than two people deciding where to have lunch. In the surreal situation, bravery and skill were needed, but craziness and luck were absolutes. Fortunately, these two had a truckload of the latter. Finally, Tyler prevailed, but even with the dogs of war on their heels, the White Wolf walked back to the car.

Once Longvue maneuvered the Justice into the Mercedes, the world returned at warp speed. Shutting the door, Tyler banged on the roof, "Go! Go! *Ici! Ici!*" But when the gray Benz drove off, so did Longvue's protection. Once again, he was standing in no man's land with nothing but

Stephen Huey

the pistol he took off the old Croat and a smile. He beat
feet and tried to cover his movement with fire. This was a
typical military maneuver; unfortunately, so were the results.

Amidst the confusion, noise, and fog of battle, the
empty snap of a misfire was deafening because it usually meant a deep six holiday for whoever was holding the
weapon. An immediate action drill fixed nothing except
Longvue's eyes on the hot barrel of an Uzi SMG that had
swung his direction. Through the smoke and chaos, one of
the gunmen, Jason Branagh, had turned his attention and
machine gun toward the hapless Texan. With bright green
eyes, long red hair, and a ruddy baby face, the 37-year-old
Irishman, Branagh, looked entirely out of place. It was
like someone mistakenly gave a gun to some goofy looking teenager. But nothing could be further from reality as
Branagh's long bloody CV attested.

Fortunately, neither luck nor fast-twitched muscle
fibers had abandoned Longvue. With almost unnatural
quickness and bullets following him every step of the way,
he was able to dive over the stone wall to join Burnwell.

To make his escape, the geezer who tried to shoot
Mihjilo ran toward one of the gunmen's Mercedes but he
didn't have a chance. Two of the assassins opened up on
him. When the rounds hit, they spun the old guy around
like a rag doll and slung him to the ground.

One of the attacker's cars burst into flames from the
hail of gunfire being laid down by Mihjilo's boys with the
AK-47s. The men inside bailed out, but were instantly cut
down like a turkey shoot.

Seeing Mihjilo's gray Mercedes flee, Branagh ordered his driver after it. This left only one carload of killers, and they took-up a fighting position near a building, attempting to keep Mihjilo's guards pinned down.

Longvue slid next to Burnwell, who was fumbling for his two-way radio as a torrent of bullets continued to impact and bounce off their crumbling wall of protection.

"Shots fired! This is CP 529. Shots fired! Shots fired!" On the other end was silence, then static, and finally, the unmistakable accent of a Pakistani voice who replied, "This is Vukovar HQ. Stand by."

Burnwell was amazed. "Stand by, my ass! This is CP 529. We are under fire. Get some troops out here now!"

A few moments passed and the voice returned.

"What is your situation?"

Somewhere in the universe all was proceeding as it should. People were interacting; transactions were happening, reciprocity—but not here. Burnwell's incredulous eyes turned to Longvue, then back to the radio. The time for words had come to an end. Keying the hand-held, he turned it toward the sound of heavy weapon exchange. After letting the sound engulf the transmission, he pulled the radio back to his lips. "Anything else?"

To their amazement, in the next moment a UN stamped, Russian BTR-80 armored personnel carrier rumbled onto the scene. But the arrival of help had nothing to do with either Burnwell's radio call or the jiffy-quick efficiency of the United Nation.

UNTAES HQ was only three blocks away from the shoot-out. And even though stray rounds had already shattered windows of the garrison bar where Russian officers were having a drink, or six, the military men inside had decided to ignore it. They did so until a piece of flying shrapnel broke a fine bottle of Belvedere Vodka. This was an outrage and totally unacceptable. A squad was dispatched immediately to put an end to the foolishness.

As the carrier turned the corner and headed toward the fight, both Mihjilo's vehicle and Branagh's black Benz slipped by it and sped away. The last carload of killers, still in the village, wasn't as fortunate.

Before the third group of assassins could escape, the UN personnel carrier turned its 7.62 coaxial machine gun onto their Mercedes. Full metal jacket slugs began to shred the soft target into pieces, as well as the occupants of the car. After the Mercedes was laid to waste, the carrier directed its fire on the young Serbs with the AKs.

Seeing the action, Longvue got on the hand-held to stop the carrier. "Ceasefire! Ceasefire! You're shooting at the wrong people!"

Fortunately, someone had heard and the gunfire stopped. Given the break they needed, Mihjilo's guards simply left. But the fleeing young Serbs were of no concern to the Russian soldiers or the UN officials who dismounted the armored carrier. In the Balkans, avoiding a fight was the exception and something happily acceded to by anyone who had been in country for more than a day.

Burnwell was on his side, motionless. Blood had soaked through the muffler tied to his leg. Longvue speedily took his own scarf and applied it to the wound.

"Mark, you all right? Mark, Mark can you hear me?"

"Jesus, Stickman, quit shouting! I'm hit in the leg, not the ears."

"Well, that's a relief, I guess." Longvue leaned back against the stone wall and lit a cigarette; "Thought you were dead, ol' boy."

"Disappointed?"

"Yeah, I ruined a perfectly good muffler on your fat-ass. Medic! Over here!"

With a full moon and a clear night, Mihjilo's gray Mercedes was able to travel at a high rate of speed with no lights. Though the fields were snow-covered, none had fallen for a few days, so the road was clear. Just three quarters of a mile back, Branagh and what was left of his crew were still giving chase in their shot-up black Benz. The assault had started with twelve heavily armed men in three vehicles and the element of surprise, but just as the Nazis had found five decades earlier, the Yugoslavs fought back, always.

Inside Mihjilo's car, the bride, groom, and Nakamura were stunned and sat in utter silence. The only sound was the undisturbed voice of the Justice using his Nokia cell phone.

"Ilok ruta, Jedno vozilo sledeći Mercedes crni."

"Ilok route, One vehicle following, Mercedes black."

Mihjilo rang off and looked at the frightened wedding couple.

"Ne budite zabrinuti, ovo je vaš dan vjenčanja!"

"Do not be troubled; this is your wedding day."

He turned his attention back outside. "Death makes no exceptions."

Racing through the village of Ilok, Mihjilo's vehicle disappeared down a side street. A few moments later, the black Mercedes entered. Looping around the center of the Serbian hamlet, they slowly tried to find the direction of their prey, but came up empty. Finally, the car stopped and Branagh and another gunman got out.

Serenity of moonlight reflected off the beautiful snow-covered township was lost on the Irishman. Lighting a smoke, he walked around to the driver's side window of the car. Meanwhile, his partner went to a beat-up Yugo parked on the street, put a slim-jim along the window seal, popped the door open, and hopped in.

"The old man couldn't have gone far," remarked Branagh in his heavy brogue, "The girl must come back. Search for that bastard a bit more, then go on to Kula. We'll wait in Vukovar."

As the black Mercedes drove away, Branagh's partner pulled up in a freshly stolen Yugo. The Irish killer got in, and they disappeared into the night.

Stopped on a side road, Justice Mihjilo was looking out the rear window while calmly awaiting his pursuers. Finally, the hired guns in the black Benz showed up. They fell in behind Mihjilo's gray Mercedes and the chase was on, just as the White Wolf wanted.

Though the streets were terribly thin, Mihjilo's auto streaked down the lane, followed closely by the black one. Turning left, the gray Mercedes took the corner too close and ran up onto the curb, violently cutting across the sidewalk. Just on their tail, the chasing car made the same corner, but stayed on the road. As the assassins' black Mercedes reached the apex of the turn, an explosion ripped their car apart. Twisted metal, burnt flesh, shards of glass, and broken bones flew in all directions. Mihjilo's car stopped and turned back toward what was left of the roasting wreckage. What happened next would have been impossible a decade ago.

No lights came on, no neighbors rushed to assist, no emergency services came to aid; nothing. Nothing happened except what there was, just another flaming casualty of a war too long.

Mihjilo watched as two armed men exited a nearby building and checked the burning hulk of steel for any survivors. With only charred remains, one of the armed fellows smiled and waved; then the two headed back inside.

This was the business of death and the White Wolf was an expert. *War without end was no answer*, he thought. But it was ten years on since the break-up of Yugoslavia and no one was ready to lay down their weapons. With his dead stare lost in the blaze, the old justice brooded on the futility of this life. There seemed to be no good options for change. Resigning to his fate once more, he turned to Nakamura. But there was something in her eyes, a mixture of horror and disappointment singular in its appearance and stirring in its effect. He knew what he had to do.

All Serbian coffee bars had a traditional setting of dark wood, heavy smoke, and bad service. Perhaps best, considering Jason Branagh and his partner weren't in a friendly mood.

"He got away and there were complications," said the angry Irish redhead over his cell phone.

On the other end, a distorted mechanical voice answered rudely. "That's never good."

"You're damn right! You said it would be a surprise! It was no surprise at all. I lost a lot of men. It's not like I can just pop down to the pub and pick up replacements."

"Hum, death," the voice said. "Even the noblest man's meat is inferior to pork. Is that all?"

Jason's rage reached a peak. "You bastard."

"I don't want to hear your problems, *boy-o*, just find the book."

"I need more than some *cute hoor*," said Branagh. "One day we should meet, face to face."

"Wouldn't be smart. Besides, I don't think you like me. Ciao," replied the emotionless voice and rang off.

In the parking area of the UN medical station near Vukovar, the wounded from the wedding celebration attack poured in at an alarming rate. Cars, horse-drawn wagons, pull carts, even wheel barrels loaded with damaged people pushed the scene across the River Styx, making the sixth level of Hell seem more orderly. Cries of pain from the injured; parents holding blood-soaked children; medical personnel running about shouting instructions; everyone trying to be the next in line; automobile horns blaring; while more and more injured bodies crammed into the confusion.

Arriving by Jeep to "take charge" of this tragedy was a 34-year-old Norwegian Army Captain named Lodvor Olsen. During his short, but brilliant, military career, he had kept impeccable paperwork, cut a fine clean figure in a great looking uniform, and had an uncle who was a member of the Storting, Supreme Legislature of Norway. In every way, or so he thought, he was just the man for the job.

Surveying the situation, the young captain became visibly displeased. He then marched his way to the front of the medical station and attempted to bring order to the chaos. Though his actions were usually ineffective, this situation was no exception.

"They're not UN," Olsen began in his best military voice, "You will stop what you're doing." But nobody stopped and nobody listened. Raising his volume, he tried again. "Only UN personnel are to be treated. All others must wait."

Regardless of his tone, not a nurse, soldier, doctor, villager, or stray dog paid the slightest bit of attention to the yelping Norwegian. With each step toward the doors of the station, his anger grew threefold. By the time the little Viking reached the front and straddled the entryway to the med station, he was ready to loose the ferocious Olsen from Oslo.

"All who are not UN are ordered to leave the area immediately," he declared sharply. Still nothing.

"You there," said the captain to four Russian soldiers. "Two of you stand guard. Allow no civilians in the station." If it weren't for the scientific fact he had mass and was taking up space, he would swear he was a voiceless ghost.

Now, the storm inside Capt. Lodvor Olsen broke through the container walls. His chubby face went blood red, his pulsating eyes bulged from their socket, and this erstwhile administrator exploded into a 'category five' hissy fit. "I said stop these people!"

Stephen Huey

Feeling more embarrassment for than duty to the hysterical young officer, two of the privates moved half-heartedly toward their assignments. The other two Russians, both sergeants, were a little less roused by the spectacle. They each lit cigarettes, gawked at the blinking generalissimo a little longer, then slowly started to corral the civilians as well. Of course, the effect was to pour even more anarchy into a sufficiently chaotic setting.

Suddenly, stretchers loaded with badly injured villagers were halted while only a few wounded UN personnel went inside the station. It was an unconscionable act. Capt. Olsen had turned the clear need for immediate humanitarian aid into an administrative board game. Fortunately, a few considered the nattering Norwegian nothing more than a quibbling psychopath.

When Olsen from Oslo spotted a petite Tunisian nurse, who continued to attend to a Serbian boy missing a leg, clearly flouting his authority, it was time to flex the Viking muscle. Stomping over, the captain was going to set accounts right.

While the mother cried hysterically, and the RN quickly bandaged what was left, Lodvor tried to pull her away, all the while shouting his mantra, "This is not authorized. I order you to cease." Had Godot finally arrived?

Nearby, piled up on a stretcher, Olsen caught sight of an ill-tempered Mark Burnwell. It was clear the American policeman had had enough of this two-bit tin-horned Scandinavian's tragicomedy. The captain was getting prepared but that fight never came. Colonel M.E. Lovejoy, chief of medical services for UNTAES, had arrived on the scene and things were about to change in a hurry.

Margaret Emma was eleventh in an unbroken line of Lovejoys serving as doctors in every British war since Napoleon. She had the pedigree, as well as the ability, and a career path that was grooming her for the top spot in the Royal Medical Service: first in her class, outstanding service record, decorated for bravery in the Falklands; then came Spandau Prison.

Though officially ruled a suicide, the death of Rudolf Hess in 1987 had left a cloud over her career. As the record stated, the last member of Adolf Hitler's inner circle hanged himself from a window bar in a small out-building at Spandau Prison and used the electric cord of the reading lamp to do it.

Assigned as his physician just two months prior, Lovejoy was the last person to see the 93-year-old Hess alive on that August day. In a bizarre twist, two hours after Hess' body was discovered, and before the scene was secured by police, the out-building burned to the ground with every piece of evidence inside. She was exonerated of any complicity by a military court, but suspicion was never erased, and her soaring career came back to earth. Still, she loved her work and refused to abandon Her Majesty's Army. Besides, this was the sum of her existence; what else was she going to do?

The next dozen years taught her an important lesson in life as a regular person. Where once her inclination was always to be the presence that filled the room, she learned the value of subtlety. A pleasing but firm nature can be disarming and sometimes far more effective than the blunt force trauma of overwhelming intellect. Now, as

Olsen the terrible was about to learn, she knew which to use when.

"What is the problem, captain?" Lovejoy immediately went to the wounded child held by the frightened mother. Lodvor offered a salute and started to decipher.

"Colonel, I explained we can't treat them here. This is for UN only."

Paying little attention to his answer, she continued, "Send this one in immediately. Why are they lined up outside? Johnson! Get these people inside!"

"Colonel, they must find their own way. It's against regulations to treat civilians in a military ambulance."

Capt. Olsen's strict attention to the regulations found no quarter with the head doctor. In less than a minute, Margaret Lovejoy turned the flow of patients back to humanity. Clearly smarting from the rebuff, and apparently having no idea what to do about it, the little Viking stood with a stern look of displeasure and folded his arms across his chest.

"Lodvor, either give me a hand or get out of the way!"

This knock must have severely wounded his Nordic pride because the disrespect was unmistakable in Capt. Olsen's voice as he shouted, "Colonel, I must protest. This is highly irregular and it must stop!"

Hastily assisting with care for the wounded, Lovejoy didn't look up. She didn't need to; her tone was crystal clear. "Come to attention, captain."

In the cosmic order of life, everyone has a turn at making bad choices. When that time comes, in most cases, one gets to choose whether it will be a large mistake or a small one. Lodvor was up. He gave it a go and went big. Foolishly, he started to walk away.

"I said, come to attention!" Repeating orders wasn't the habit of Col. Margaret E. Lovejoy. Her booming command snapped Olsen erect and motionless. And it was there he stayed while the business of care and compassion finally got back on track.

"Good job, Lodvor," said Burnwell with a Cheshire cat-size grin as he was carried past the stationary captain. "I think you've got her right where you want."

In short order, the scene outside the medical station changed from bedlam to sanity. Returning to the petrified Norwegian stick, Lovejoy asked, "Do the rules apply to everyone except you?"

"Ma'am?" Lodvor grunted, who appeared barely able to hold his temper.

"Hypocrisy captain, it wears the fool well." Leaving him locked in his position, she walked toward the building. At the door, she contemplated leaving the young Norwegian there for the night, but shook her head and entered. "Dismissed!"

With every bed in the emergency room taken, Burnwell was stretched across a desktop sporting his newly bandaged leg. Lovejoy and a nurse arrived, and the doctor went through her usual seamless checks: chart, pulse, fever.

"American policemen, hum. Looks like bullets bounce off. How are you feeling?"

"Better for seeing you."

"Don't push your luck, Yank."

Dr. Margaret and her assistant went to the next patient, but Burnwell didn't stop.

"So, Doc, you come here often?"

Not answering him, Maggie continued on her way. Never one to be put off by rejection, Mark reclined and thought out loud. "Don't push your luck–Yank! Yeah, there's a double meaning in that; she's crazy about me."

Next on her rounds, the colonel arrived at the side of the old Croatian who tried to shoot Mihjilo. Though riddled with bullet holes, somehow he was still alive and able to latch firmly onto Dr. Lovejoy's arm. With all he had left, he pulled her down to his face and started speaking in a low scratchy tone. At first she was surprised the aged chap could talk. That gave way to the fact it was in excellent English, but the most astonishing thing was the story itself. From his tone she knew he was determined to tell what he knew before leaving this earth, and he did. When finished, he let loose of her arm as well as his soul.

Lovejoy rose but kept her gaze locked in the Croat's dead, dark eyes.

Stillness.

Then the world rushed back. The doctor checked for a pulse, but found nothing. Taking the bed sheet in hand, Maggie pulled it over his head all the while considering the strange declaration she had just heard. "Call for the priest."

chapter

THREE

"NATO is backed into a corner. They have no choice but to start the bombing. The Serbs are overrunning Kosovo's army," emphatically stated the short, round, and balding senior State Department Officer, Charles A. Baxter III. Shaking his drink and unconvinced by the argument, Stephen R. A. Truman, Chief of UNTAES, countered his old friend's point with a baited trap.

"Not long ago, the Kosovo Liberation Army was a terrorist organization. Are they now what your government calls freedom fighters?" With the snare set, Truman, a rather clever Zambian lawyer by trade, simply let the Balkans' expert walk into his setup.

"Policies change, Stephen. Ethnic cleansing by the Serbs has pushed it in the other direction."

"Ethnic cleansing! I see. And what of Rwanda, Chuck? Ethnic cleansing seems to have had a field day there. Will policies change?"

"One disaster at a time, Stephen."

One disaster at a time, thought Truman as he nodded to his longtime confederate recalling how they met. *No phrase better encapsulates our relationship.*

Their friendship started thirty years ago in Lusaka, Zambia when Truman and Baxter literally ran into each other. Both were attending the Non-Alignment Movement, NAM, Summit as representatives of their countries in 1970, when Charles rammed the front of Stephen's car in the parking lot of the conference hall. Organized during the Cold War, as a middle course for nations, NAM straddled the warring Western and Eastern blocs and represented a means of peaceful coexistence. But the lofty idea had little merit for the young Truman while he stared at the smashed grill of his red drop-top 1967 Ford Corsair.

It had taken three years and a loan to purchase; therefore, replacing it was simply out of the question. To compound an already bad situation, having it repaired in Zambia was highly questionable. So, there he was, just him, a steaming hunk of twisted metal, and some weird looking short American.

This was Charles Baxter's first solo assignment for the State Department. He was there in Lusaka to make friends for the U.S. But in three short days he'd offended the wife of India's Prime Minister with an off-color joke, spilled a drink on the uniform of Egypt's leading Military Attaché, and now, crashed his vehicle into one of Zambia's young diplomats. The first two mishaps were enough to have him sent home immediately but he did make the third one right.

Charles arranged to have Stephen's auto repaired and, over time, paid for it in full. Along the way they developed a genuine friendship, which cemented into a lasting bond. So, when Stephen Truman was tapped by the United Nations for the top spot in the Yugoslavian peacekeeping mission, his first choice to help with this wreck-of-a-country was his old friend Chuck.

There was a knock at Truman's open office door. Looking up, the Chief saw, what he called, the extraordinary UNTAES lawyers and waved them in. He considered the pair extraordinary, not so much for their skills, though both were capable, but because they looked to him as if they had been plucked from Hollywood's central casting and sent to the mission.

Nikita Zavisha and Claire Anjou, a Russian and a French/Canadian respectively, were the kind of people whom most people imagine as on the cover of *People* magazine. In short, these were two really good-looking people.

Zavisha, believed to be former KGB or so everyone in the mission romanticized, couldn't have appeared to be more so; tall, muscular, something straight out of a John le Carré Cold War thriller. Even more striking was his peculiar ability to turn a phrase in English. When a heavy Russian accent spits out a line like, *a didactic perspicaciousness to illuminate;* more than a few native speakers were stumped. His ability and reputation were formidable, particularly in comparison to that of his colleague, Claire Anjou.

Being a drop-dead gorgeous, green-eyed black woman wasn't the handicap for Anjou; it was her story. At present, she held a top legal assignment in UN Peacekeeping Operations. Prior to this, she was employed as a junior public defender in the backwater of Quebec's Provincial Courts. With a CV so remarkably thin upon the ground, mission cocktail chatter, which spread like free drinks at a lodge meeting, assumed she did her best work on her back. But assumptions are what they are.

"The situation is under control by soldiers and police. You'll receive a full report before morning," said Zavisha. "But, interesting news. The gunmen were attempting to kill the one, Justice Kulas Mihjilo. He was attending a wedding."

Baxter and Truman were dumbfounded. Saying Mihjilo was seen attending some small village marriage ceremony was like saying the Pope had been seen having a shake at Dairy Queen. "How extraordinary," Truman answered. "Are you sure?"

"Reasonably certain," declared the big Russian heading directly for the bar which graced the corner of Truman's cramped office. Alcohol was a common denominator in UN mission life and pervasive. Few offices were large enough to formalize it; most just had a bottle of *moonlight* in their desk drawer. Yet, views on drinking alcohol, once as universally accepted in a war zone as smoking, had started to take a curious turn for some groups in the mission. At the nearby United States military contingent, for instance, liquor was banned because command thought it bad for the soldier's health. Yet, greasy fast food like Pop-eye's Fried Chicken and Burger King was readily available. Seemed it was okay to be fat, but not a fat drunk.

"Well, that's just dandy," grumbled Baxter. "I suppose they'll try carpet-bombing for his birthday next week. You said attempt. Was anyone hurt, Nikita?"

"Yes. Last update, fifteen are dead and thirty wounded, including an American policeman."

"His name?" Truman asked, concerned.

Nervously, Anjou looked through her notes. "Mark, Mark Burnwell. He received a leg wound, umh, it's not serious." Seeing Anjou was a bit jumpy, Zavisha motioned to the fifth of Stolichnaya Elit. "Yes, Nikita, please."

"What is it with this guy? Seems like someone tries to kidnap or kill him every week."

"Charles, it's the book, no less."

In mock surprise, the sardonic American gave a swift rejoinder. "Ah, of course, Mr. Zavisha. The book; the one with the treasure map. Ahg!"

"Do you know of anyone who has seen this 'book,' or for that matter, the treasure?"

"No, Stephen, only the most official Serbian anecdote," said Zavisha. "But real or no, they kill for it."

Baxter got up and walked to the window. "Turkish gold, Hapsburg diamonds, sure; might as well add Madonna's bedroom key and give this fairy tale some juice." Keeping his gaze outside, he continued, "And what about you, Ms. Anjou? Do you believe Mihjilo has a book leading to the Yugoslavian bonanza?"

"I believe, I mean, the Balkans are full of mysteries, sir."

"And suckers. There's no Hapsburg treasure in the mountains of Sarajevo; it's all a myth. It grew up around Marshall Tito because it helped him with his creditors. There is a book, though; a book of accounts, and Mihjilo has it. But it runs straight through the mountains of Switzerland to the bank."

Anjou joined Truman at the table as Zavisha arrived with the drinks.

"Charles, you seem well informed. Is this something we need to discuss?"

"Perhaps we should, Stephen," Baxter said as he walked to the bar. Whiskey followed by a splash of soda fizzed amply in the Waterford crystal tumbler Charles held. He studied it for a moment, then started his report.

"In the early 1970s, the U.S. eased tensions with Yugoslavia and allowed trade. A Yugoslav company, Borovo Shoes, set up offices in the states. Mihjilo's son, Josip, ran the operation until the mid 80s."

"Did the shoes do any better than the cars?" asked Anjou.

"You kidding? The company was never meant to make a profit. It was a shell for the conduit between the U.S. and Yugoslavia. People, information, and money—a lot of money, went through Borovo Shoes."

"And when Tito died, the shell; it crumbled?"

"Yes and no, Nikita. The apparatus fell apart, but there was, and still are, millions of dollars, to which Justice Mihjilo holds the purse strings. The funds are being used to supply the Serbs with weapons. And I just don't understand it."

Baxter took down a framed chalk drawing of the iconic war-damaged Vukovar Water Tower, which hung next to the large single office window. It was artistic handy-work of his own doing and he admired it for a moment. "He's an old man, he has the money; why doesn't he just leave?"

"Courage is the first of human qualities because it is the quality that guarantees all the others," quipped Zavisha.

"Winston Churchill?"

Annoyed at being recognized so quickly, the Russian conceded, "You're correct, Mr. Truman."

"Well said, and I agree," the Zambian continued. "Mihjilo is fighting for his homeland, his people. He isn't going to abandon either."

"Just what we need, a patriot," retorted Charles. "He's fighting a war that has already been decided."

"To some, perhaps," said Zavisha.

"The killing in Kosovo is brutal and senseless. Its been decided," Baxter said. He re-hung his drawing and turned his attention back outside the window. "I came to Yugoslavia in 1969. At that time these folks were just hard to understand. Thirty years later, they're a complete mystery. How is Mihjilo anyway?"

"Uhm, we don't know," Anjou offered gently. "He and a few others, all unidentified, fled shortly after the shooting started. But the military and police have been contacted."

Stephen Huey

"Don't waste your time. Better odds finding the trea-sure before finding him," groused Baxter.

"I'm sure you're right. Mihjilo was Tito's most clever Partisan, the White Wolf. You've heard stories, yes?"

"More times than I care to remember. Nikita, he's an old fool, fighting for no good reason."

"It is the primary right of men to die and kill for the land they live in, and to punish with exceptional severity all members of their own race who have warmed their hands at the invaders' hearth." The eloquent summation quieted the room and all heads turned toward the placid Zambian lawyer. "Seems Nikita and I both read Mr. Churchill."

Kula, Serbia

An AM radio sent the low and sad complaint of a Serbian folk song drifting through the small dark restau-rant. Mihjilo and Nakamura had the place to themselves, with the exception of the three armed guards who covered the front, back, and side doors.

Poor electrical lighting, candles, and a warming fire-place gave the room a sense of sanctuary. The walls were filled with common scenes of an agrarian homeland, but for two singular exceptions, an old black-and-white pho-tograph of Tito and a copy of an ancient painting by Pieter Brueghel, "*Landscape with the Fall of Icarus.*"

Nakamura lit a cigarette with a candle and moved closer to inspect the painting. Mihjilo gave her a glass of well-aged cabernet sauvignon and joined her.

"As a boy, I helped to make this wine. It comes from Erdut, my village. I was sixteen when I left. Many summers have come and gone." He raised his broad bowl cruet to her. *"Zivjeli."* They touched glasses in salute and returned to the painting.

"You have taste, Ms. Nakamura. It's one of my finest copies, Brueghal's Fall of Icarus."

"No plough stops for the man who dies."

"You know the work, I'm most impressed."

"In school, I found mythology much more interesting than the cytoskeleton." Smiling, she took another sip of the excellent vintage. "And my grades reflected it."

The youngest of four children, Kazuko Rita Nakamura was the only girl, the only half Japanese, half American, and the only one who went her own way. Her older half-brothers, from her father's first marriage to a Japanese woman, were all doctors with the United Nations, just like their father. Even Kazuko's mother, born and raised in the Bronx, was a registered nurse. But halfway through her first semester of pre-med at Johns Hopkins, Kazuko went to a party at Saint John's College in Annapolis and never wanted to come back.

One of the few "Great Books Programs" still in operation, a St. John's student read and discussed the works of Western Civilization's most prominent contributors in philosophy, theology, mathematics, science, poetry, music, and literature. But "Johnnies," as they called themselves, didn't take tests; they were evaluated on the papers they wrote and their participation in class lectures. In fact, grades A through F were given, but only released at the request of the student. Supposing her conservative workaday parents would allow and pay for her to receive a Bachelor of Arts degree through such peculiar and elegant means was correct; they pushed her all the way through to a Master of Arts.

Visibly pleased with their common interest, Mihjilo beamed for a moment. But pleasure was short-lived as the melancholy demands of the present returned. "Ms. Nakamura, I need your help. We have little time so I shall be direct. I have a son in Zagreb. He claims otherwise, but no matter, he's my son. I have no other family, and now, no one to trust, no one but you."

Next, the old Serb produced a small book covered in well-worn black leather from the inside pocket of his jacket, which he gave to her. On first inspection, Kazuko found the book unremarkable. It was a tiny thing, not much larger than one's palm. But a closer look denoted two unusual features; there was a faded imprint of a three-headed wolf on its cover and the inside pages were filled with row upon row of numbers and letters.

"Please, give this to my son. Give it only to him and tell no one you have it."

"What is this?"

"My legacy. The words are a great puzzle, but my son has the key."

"No, you can't give up. Come back with me, Justice Mihjilo. We'll give you protection."

"As tonight? No, my dear, the time, it's done for two reasons that will never change. First, we Serbs made our choices long ago. Building our nation is the work of my lifetime, something not easily altered. Second, I carry a cancer inside me which can not be cured."

Seeing the concern that filled her eyes touched the old soldier, but nothing would change his course.

"Please, don't mistake my reflections. My confession isn't self-serving, only fact. I seek neither your pity nor your protection." Mihjilo finished his glass and took a seat near the fire. "Come sit."

Nakamura joined him, and he poured more wine for them both. "The man who tried to kill me tonight has been trying since 1960. Goran Poljak; I thought him dead. All these years he's wanted the same thing, that book. Well, he can no longer have it, but I can no longer keep it." Mihjilo reached across the table and took her hand. "Without fail, you must get this book to my son, Josip. I know it's hard for you to understand."

Hard to understand; that may be the understatement of the year, reckoned Kazuko. She knew Josip Mihjilo, the White Wolf's only son, was one of the leading figures in the push for the break-up of Yugoslavia. He had joined the Croatian government at the outset of the civil war, taking a position in the ministry of justice, and remained a staunch supporter of Croatian independence. This war had pitted son against father, but what she didn't know was that the old Mihjilo was ready for a change.

"A mad man rules Serbia, Slobodan Milosevic, and I can no longer be a part of it." The aged Serbian fighter wasn't mincing words and got straight to the point.

"My son leads a faction that is seeking re-unification between the Serbs and Croats. They must be given a chance. Therefore, you must get this book to my son without fail. And when you do, tell him these words, precisely ... *in death, the one is now three as they return to their mother.* You must remember exactly as I tell you. Now, say."

Nakamura repeated the phrase dutifully. An odd line, *in death, the one is now three as they return to their mother.* But as she would learn, nothing in her life measured to this singular event and this strange little phrase.

"Excellent, most excellent; and don't worry, Josip will understand. It is done, Aleksander!"

Mihjilo stood, picked up the book, and handed it to her. He closed her hands around the binding to silently affirm her task. She rubbed the cover as if to make sure it was real and quickly placed it inside her coat as the guard entered.

"Idu u Vukovar, bude bezbedna ona je sve!"
"Go to Vukovar, be safe she is everything"

Not knowing what to say, she kissed him on the cheek and left abruptly with her escort. After their departure, the White Wolf poured another glass of the dark red cab and raised it high to the man on the wall. "I left my village in 1939 to carry a rifle for my country. I carry it still."

Across the street from the restaurant and concealed in shadows, a young thug smoked and watched the front of Mihjilo's place. A few moments later, a banged-up Yugo rolled in behind him. Inside were Jason Branagh and his three-man crew. Branagh got out and waved the young street brawler over.

"You sure they're in there?"

"Would I be here?"

"Fair enough. How many?"

"Wrong question, Boss. How much?"

"Give the right answers and you won't need anything for a long time, *boy-o.*"

"We have deal, Boss. There are the three men, a woman, and old bastard Mihjilo."

"Good job. Jimmy, give this man something for his trouble."

Leaning down to the open window on the driver's side of the Yugo, the callow tough guy greedily awaited his payoff, and he got it. A Russian made PB 9mm pistol with a silencer planted itself firmly on his forehead and thumped and punched the Serbian hooligan backwards and dead into the snow. Not considering the lifeless youth a second longer, Branagh stepped over the body and gave his men concise instructions.

Moments later, Nakamura and Aleksander exited the rear of the restaurant; they got into the gray Mercedes and disappeared without illuminating their headlights. As Aleksander's car turned the corner and out of sight, the crummy Yugo arrived at the opposite end of the parking lot. Branagh and the others quickly piled out and entered the building, unopposed. Inside, the owner had set a hypnologic scene for his much-expected visitors.

After Mihjilo dismissed the other guards, he turned up the volume on the static-filled music, opened another bottle of wine, and waited tranquilly. Where once the full measure of life in its spring and summer had filled this room, now there was only a single winter's memory alone near the fire. When Branagh and another man crashed into the room, the White Wolf gave them no notice. They were expected, and the preparations had long been made. As the intruders advanced toward him, the old wolf kept his eyes on the flames.

"Take the others and search the building," Branagh commanded while keeping his eyes fixed on his target by the fire. With his pistol at the ready, the Irish killer moved slowly toward Mihjilo. "I could shoot you now, old man."

"Yes, but no matter; it's too late. The flames take what you seek."

Looking into the fireplace, Branagh saw a small black book engulfed by fire. Jason sprinted over and kicked it out but the book was destroyed.

"Lying bastard, you gave it to the Japanese girl."

"Perhaps. I'm old, I forget. You could be right."

Finally, Mihjilo turned to his would-be killer. "But you'll never know." As the radio coughed out the sound of a mournful fiddle strangling some ancient tune, their cold eyes met.

Suddenly, the heavy sound of racing footsteps preceded Branagh's man bursting into the room and heading for the exit. "Get out! There's a bomb!"

In magnificent serenity, the end well played, Mihjilo raised his glass to the fleeing assassins and returned to his fire. As Branagh dived through the front window, a powerful explosion ripped through the building.

The force of the blast hurled Branagh over the elevated porch and headfirst into the glazed snow on the front yard. A deluge of glass, curtains, pieces of furniture, chunks of building, and bloody body parts followed. A large section of the café was completely obliterated and what remained of the structure cooked in an angry blaze. Branagh's accomplice, now dead, mangled, and burning, hung half out of a window. Amazingly, two things survived, the radio that still bleated tired Serbian folk music and a semi-conscious Irishman, Jason Branagh.

chapter

FOUR

UNTAES Headquarters, Vukovar: Daily Briefing
Room

If ever the well-being of nationalism, vanity, and
pretense were in question, a spin through the daily brief
would quickly cure such skepticism. A peacock ball provided less ostentation than presented at the gathering. *Every* member from *every* country wore *every* decoration that
his or her uniform allowed or could be crammed onto the
breastplate. With the exception of civilians who would
sneak a ribbon on a lapel from time to time, the room
was awash in splendiferous UN khaki, military, and po-

Stephen Huey

lice costumes; an apotheosis of pomposity, not to mention great theatre.

Seated at the head of a U-shaped table was Truman, flanked by Lovejoy, Zavisha, Anjou, Baxter, Longvue, and several others. Across the room, delivering the daily intelligence summary, was Natalie Davis. At first glance, her continental attire coupled with long black hair, deep blue eyes, and sharp attractive features pegged her as European, but then Davis spoke. After a few words from the Department of State political officer, the unmistakable twang of a Texas accent shattered the illusion. But eccentric didn't begin to define this woman from Big D.

To most of the world, Dallas, TX was viewed as a vibrant international metropolis. But to Natalie, the prairie city was just one big hard-right, good-ole-boy, come-to-Jesus, never-ending-gun-show of an outpost. So, after college, she immediately joined the State Department and volunteered to go anywhere, anytime, at any danger. The folks at State didn't let her down. Her first two stops were Phnom Penh and Ouagadougou. Exotic, yes; harsh, certainly, but nothing matched the next post.

In early 1994, Natalie arrived in Kigali, Rwanda shortly before the assassination of Rwandan President Juvenal Habyarimana on April 6th and the start of an unspeakable genocide. During the following 100 days, Rwandan military and Hutu militia murdered more than half a million Tutsis people. Primarily these victims were hacked to death by machete because rifles were too expensive.

Davis was one of the last Americans to be evacuated from the nightmare in Kigali and she was sent to a place most would consider a welcome change, Bordeaux, France. But the beauty of the countryside and the luxury of the city were lost on her. It was all boredom; boredom so profound it pushed her to make twelve requests for transfer in nine months as well as mastering the art of rolling her own cigarettes. In a strange sense, her persistence was rewarded with first a move to Zagreb, Croatia, then to the teeth of the Balkan war, Vukovar.

"Police monitors said that the explosion occurred around 2:30 AM. As of this morning, the remains of two men have been found. One has been positively identified as Justice Kulas Mihjilo." Reaction to the news was muted for two reasons. First, the rumor of his death had been circulating all morning. And second, no one knew what it meant.

"Natalie, do we have any idea who did this?" asked Charles Baxter in his well-nurtured disdain for all Yugoslavian intrigue.

"Nothing certain, but Serb officials in Belgrade are blaming the CIA."

"Well, why not? Those guys haven't been fingered in years. Have they finished searching the site?" Baxter quizzed.

"I called just before the meeting. They're still working."

"And what of Ms. Nakamura?"

"She's still missing, Mr. Truman."

"Thank you, Ms. Davis." Stephen Truman rose and continued, "Unfortunately, I have more bad news. The morning report indicates Serb troops have not reversed their course in Kosovo. Therefore, we must assume a NATO attack is imminent. So, until further notice, all non-critical travel is suspended. I also want to see all department heads here at 10:00 AM to review evacuation procedures. Ladies and gentlemen, thank you."

A grim sense of urgency elevated the chatter in the room as people broke off into small groups. Margaret Lovejoy made a beeline to the front of the table and took Truman by the arm.

"Stephen, do you have a moment? Last night there was a rather remarkable incident. I was tending to an old Croatian brought into the emergency room." As she expounded on the previous evening's events, her voice trailed off out of earshot of the others.

Osijek, Croatia

Longvue entered his apartment carrying two bags of groceries and headed straight for the kitchen. In the few steps from the front door to the cookery, it was a journey through old world effectiveness, cold war austerity, and new age technology. There was an antique heating system of fire and bricks, which warmed the room sparsely populated with straight-line uncomfortable 1960s Hungarian furniture. Near the front window was a VCR/CD player with all the latest movies and music pirated in Romania. Though neat and clean, the place was a swirling cultural catastrophe with the exception of two anchor points.

The first was on a side table next to the only agreeable chair in the place, a 1930s edition of the *Complete Sherlock Holmes*. As pronounced on the aged cover, it was, "Every adventure of fiction's most fascinating detective," and Tyler's closest friend.

Dog-eared and marked-up, Longvue had been reading and re-reading the stories for a decade since the book was given to him by the owner of a furniture store who had been using it as a display item that he wanted rid of.

The second mainstay was prominently displayed on top of the television. It was a 5 x 7 photo of him and Nakamura near the Pallas Athene Fountain in front of the Austrian Parliament building. The two were in Vienna attending a winter conference when a few of them slipped away during a particularly boring session, and someone in the group snapped the picture. For Longvue, it was the spot where he learned two fascinating things about his Japanese/American friend, their common interest in Sherlock Holmes stories and just what it meant to have a St. John's education.

While standing in front of the Athene Fountain, Nakamura launched into a forty-five-minute explanation of who the goddess Athena was and why she was atop the watercourse. Long before she finished, the group decided that if they were going to be bored, they would rather be inside and warm than outside and cold. So, everyone returned to the conference, everyone except Longvue. He stayed because he thought she was lovely; an egghead yes, but cute nonetheless. Then the magic happened.

Seeing that her audience had dwindled to one, Kazuko realized she had done it again. Having a detailed knowledge of Greek Mythology doesn't exactly make one fun at parties. But to be so young, she was comfortable in her skin. Knowing her lecture had sent the others packing, she quipped to her single companion, "But he had not the supreme gift of the artist, the knowledge of when to stop."

To this, Longvue tilted his head like a confused dog for a moment, then brightened with his recollection and said, "I know that quote. It's from Sherlock Holmes."

"*The Norwood Builder*," she replied in a tone like everyone in the world had an encyclopedic familiarity with the writings of Sir Arthur Conan Doyle. From that point, their friendship was sealed.

After a few moments, Tyler came from the kitchen with a freshly made cup of coffee in one hand while balancing his hat and coat in the other. Pitching the winter gear on the dining room table, he took a cigarette from his breast pocket and tossed the pack of Marlboros on the tabletop. There was a knock at his front door.

"Oh, hell," Longvue said. He assumed it was his landlady, again. Since repairing her washing machine a few weeks ago, he had become 'the man around the house.' Now, if there was a light bulb that needed to be changed or trash to take out, she came knocking. Standing stock still and silent, he lit his smoke and waited for her to leave.

There were three more knocks, each a bit louder than the last. Still, he did nothing. The knocks changed to hard bangs, three of them in rapid succession.

"Tyler, it's me! Open up, please!"

Longvue quickly recognized the voice, leaped over the couch in one bound, and opened the door to find a wide-eyed Nakamura.

"Kazuko, where have you been?"

Not saying a word, she entered hastily and closed the door behind her. Immediately, she went to the window, pulled the curtains shut, and fidgeted about the room before turning to her friend.

"Tyler, I'm scared."

"You're fine now. Don't worry."

"No, you don't understand. We have to leave. I'm sure I was followed, they'll be here soon."

"Who'll be here soon?"

Exhausted from the long night, Nakamura took a seat. She pulled a cigarette from the pack on the table and Longvue extended his lighter. She bent down slightly to the flame, lit it, and settled back, exhaling a smoke cloud in what appeared to be relief. Then Longvue noticed her eyes were locked on the framed photograph on the television. This was the first time in his diggings, and it was obvious she hadn't expected to see an image of herself so notably displayed. A bit embarrassed, Longvue positioned himself between her and the photo. He cleared his throat and got back to the matter at hand as to why she was there in the first place. "Okay, what's going on? Who's following you?"

"I don't have time to explain. You're going to have to trust me. I must go to Zagreb. And I was hoping that you would come with me."

"Zagreb? What's in Zagreb? I can't go to Zagreb."

The screeching shrill whistle of the 10:55 from Osijek to Zagreb split the icy morning air. Nakamura and Longvue exited the station, ran along the platform, and jumped on-board the departing train just in time. Finding an empty compartment, the couple entered and sat in silence. Picking up a discarded newspaper, Longvue read

Stephen Huey

while Kazuko studied her companion and smiled. Turning her gaze outside, she thought, *so much for 'I can't go to Zagreb.'*

UNTAES Headquarters, Vukovar: Office of Stephen Truman

"His killer was an Irishman, working for the CIA! What the bloody hell," exclaimed Zavisha in a tone suggesting he found Lovejoy's pronouncement a bit hard to swallow even by Balkan standards.

"Nikita, I should think you would be the least surprised by this news."

The heated discussion between the Russian lawyer, the English doctor, and the American bureaucrat about Mihjilo's death had been playing out for over an hour. Sitting at his desk, far from the bout at the conference table, the UN Chief listened and watched the contest. His head constantly turned from one person to the next in strange fascination as the trio batted points, counterpoints, and wisecracks, back and forth.

"These are the words of a crazy, dying Croat," Nikita continued. "Of course we should have full faith and confidence in his statement!"

"Doctor, did he say anything else about the Irishman?"

"No, Charles. The only other thing he mentioned was a book with a three-headed wolf on the cover."

As if choreographed for a community theatre play, Zavisha, Baxter, and Truman all did the classic double-take when Margaret spouted this singular and most significant detail.

"That's it! That's the book. Did he say he'd seen it?"

"Yes, Charles. That is what I have been trying to tell you two 'learned' gentlemen for the past hour!"

"Perhaps Belgrade was right; maybe the CIA did kill him," Baxter said.

"Or IRA, or KGB, or do-re-mi," quipped Zavisha, in a voice unconvinced. "Why is there always the conspiracy? No! It's simple. There is the book, yes. The book leads to a lot of money. Someone wants the book, not government, not terrorist, some 'one' person. That's all! The rest is circus."

All went quiet.

Zavisha's passionate summation, for the moment, had put a cap on the exhaustive report about the White Wolf. But there were still plenty of holes in the story, and everyone knew it.

Rising from his desk, Truman went to the window and observed security personnel outside UN HQ busily preparing for a possible evacuation. "Nikita, I see you've made your point. Unfortunately, none of you have solved the primary matter, finding Ms. Nakamura."

Showing they had neither the answer nor the will to continue, both Zavisha and Lovejoy rose from their chairs.

"Excuse, please. There are some phone calls I must take," the big Russian mumbled as he exited the room.

"I'm taxed as well, Stephen," Lovejoy said while being less abrupt in her departure. She pushed her chair to the conference table and walked to the door. "I'll leave you two to hatch your schemes."

Stephen Huey

After the office door was pulled shut, Truman and
Baxter were left staring at each other, expressionless. A
confused silence lingered between them for a few moments, then Baxter broke the spell.

"How long have you known Zavisha?"

"Since my arrival; why do you ask?"

"You know his background?

"Yes, but I assume you mean to tell me more, Chuck?"

chapter

FIVE

UNTAES Headquarters, Vukovar: Office of Nikita Zavisha

In the field, UN office space was erected with oblong reinforced metal boxes looking similar to ocean shipping containers. Because of their shape and stacking arrangement, it made the UN HQ compound look as if some giant child had snapped together an assemblage of white Legos.

Most offices were shared and about the size of a large closet; just enough room for two desks, two chairs, and two thoughts. Fortunately, Zavisha had a private space, which was not only good for him, but also for smoking meat.

Nikita Spiridon Zavisha had been a two-pack-a-day man since his days as a stevedore on the docks of Novorossiysk, which would have been his life if not for excelling in academics, deftly avoiding political landmines in the Soviet Army, and making the right "friends" in the First Chief Directorate. In fact, it was this blend of education, refinement, and being a step away from the proletariat that made the big Russian so good at his moonlighting job. But when the Soviet machine finally dropped dead and opportunities to make money were suddenly on the increase, Nikita leaped from eastern *apparatchik* to western capitalist with such alacrity Adam Smith may have twitched in his grave.

Zavisha entered the room and sat at the desk chair only to find himself confronted with the agglomeration of information he always piled on the desktop; several thick UN studies covering disease, human trafficking, drugs, etc.; dozens of daily status reports from police, courts and prisons; policy briefs, personal letters, newspapers and two well-thumbed books for recreational reading, *The Rise and Fall of the Third Reich* and *Black Lamb and Grey Falcon*. Without complication, and in a single motion, he snatched the paper he needed from the midst of the storm on his workspace.

After digging further into the pile, he found the phone and dialed the number written on the sheet, but the connection didn't work. He hung up, dialed again, but again no connection. Zavisha lit a cigarette and tried again, again the same. Frustration came standard with every eastern European phone.

Anjou came to the doorway and paused, watching the Russian wrestle with the phone. Being so animated, his performance never failed to entertain. With a smile she knocked lightly.

In his usual quick manner, Zavisha looked up, waved her in, and continued to dial feverishly. The call didn't connect despite his persistence and he slammed down the phone.

"The brief on the Udvar crossing into Hungary, the meeting is in an hour," said Anjou as she placed the folder on the summit of Zavisha's mountain of paper.

"The border is a Swiss Cheese. Claire, agreement is already done; we have what is required."

"Then I wasted my time?"

"No, you've fulfilled the obligation. It's right."

"Nikita, I find your sense of justice to be mercurial in its broadest sense, eloquent, swift, and thievish. I thought it was our job to ensure equity, yet it seems anything of worth is already controlled, is that right? Is that what's required? Like the book belonging to Mihjilo?"

"What do you know of this?"

"What everyone knows. But if there is treasure, it belongs to the people of this country, this region."

"Yes, Claire, that is, that is noble, yes."

"And it's right as well."

"No, that's foolish. The book belongs to those with the power and will to take it. *Realpolitik,* Claire."

In a twist of fate, the telephone rang. Not wanting to miss the miracle of a functioning phone call, Nikita instantly retrieved the receiver.

"Hello?"

"Comrade," returned the tired voice of Longvue, "I need your help."

"Ah, Comrade," Zavisha started to say Tyler's name, but quickly reconsidered because of Claire. "Where are you?"

"Zagreb with Kazuko. Nikita, I need you to contact Josip Mihjilo and arrange a meeting for us."

"Uhmm! Zagreb. And what do you have to tell him?"

"I'd rather not say over the phone, but I think you know."

Zavisha's mind started to race. *Does he have the book? Why speak to Josip? Is this a trick? Is he being forced? Claire has the figure most beautiful.*

"Nikita, you there?"

"Yes. Yes, I will do this. Your number, yes, I have it, *ciao.*"

Zavisha rang off, studied his cigarette for a moment, then cut his eyes in a slant back to Anjou.

Another ubiquitous white UN Jeep Cherokee traveled along a narrow road near the border that separated the dubious United Nations Transitional Administration in Eastern Slavonia (UNTAES) from the rest of the world. The disputed area was a queer sort of arrangement, and it clearly indicated that the Croatians got the better end of the "peace deal."

The arrangement allowed for a finger of sovereign Croatia to jut through the middle of UNTAES, which effectively broke it into two pieces, north and south. With the Serbs being primarily in the southern part of UNTAES, if they wanted to travel north they had two choices.

The first was to take a twelve-mile shortcut across the Republic of Croatia, which meant being continually harassed and probably assaulted. The second was to swing around the edge of the Croatian Republic, making the round trip some 170 miles long.

In effect, the Croats were doing all they could to make life a living hell for their Serb neighbors. Of course, they justified their cruelty with the memory of Serbian barbarity in the war. But in reality both sides were guilty of wickedness, not to mention the Muslims. Balkan history was a twisted savage tale built on death, revenge, and mystery. Inside the Jeep the inscrutability only continued.

"Do you know where we're headed?"

"Sure, Mark, it's right here on the map."

"No. Do you know how dangerous it is in Tenja?"

From the passenger seat, Natalie Davis was looking lovingly into the eyes of Mark Burnwell.

"Sweetheart, I don't have time for this. But tonight, we'll have a glass of wine and discuss the many conundrums that fill your silly man's head."

Burnwell stopped the Jeep.

"No, this is nuts. Nobody just goes to Tenja, not without the 82nd Airborne. Now what the hell is going on?"

"I was going to tell you sooner, but it doesn't make any difference now. I'm meeting with Sasha Leskovac."

"Stop! You're having a meeting with one of the ten most wanted criminals in Yugoslavia? I've been chasing that guy for six months, and now we're having a drink with him?"

"Yes, doll-face. And you've been doing an excellent job, by the way."

Davis knew she had a fight on her hands, so she rolled a cigarette and prepared for battle.

"Natalie, look at me; Leskovac is a major thug and he's holed up in that Serbian fortress called Tenja. Every man, woman, and child in that village has a weapon and a bad attitude. Everybody knows that."

"You're right; everybody knows that."

"I don't get it."

"Mark, Leskovac hasn't been captured because he gives us valuable information."

"You've been telling him my every move?"

Davis nodded in affirmation.

"So, what does that make you, Natalie?"

"Complicated?"

"You mean for half-a-year I've been chasing my tail?"

"He's an asset, Mark; he works for us."

"Asset? You mean, like a secret agent?"

"That's exactly what I mean," deadpanned Davis as she lit her smoke and cracked open the window.

"Why did you ask me to come? I'm a cop, not a spook."

"Because we're out of time. I've told Leskovac you work for us, but you've come so close to catching him, he thinks I'm lying."

"Natalie, you *are* lying."

"And doing a damn good job! But you're making it difficult. I thought cops were lazy, but no, here you come, Mr. Law & Order. So, we're going to have a drink, get some information, and show him that *we* are on the same team! Don't screw it up."

Cracking an incredulous smile, Mark asked, "Do I have a choice?"

"No."

A few seconds passed in silence.

"Natalie Davis, Natalie Davis. Probably not even your real name. I knew you were a spy."

"Just start the car and drive."

Upon arrival in the small Serbian village of Tenja, one would think it a step back to some long ago time. Though being on the border of the hotly disputed territory, the scene inside the village was the very stamp of an Arcadian life. Charming arrangements of picturesque brick houses with snow-covered tops, smoke-puffed chimneys, and neatly shoveled sidewalks blended seamlessly with the well-maintained natural surroundings. It was the picture postcard of a storybook Serbian hamlet, almost idyllic. Almost.

In one of the many horrifying episodes of the war, neighbor turned against neighbor in a small section of this community. Flames of pure hate stoked high by the leaders on both sides sent one resident next door to revenge a half-century old score between their relatives. It started with a fist fight, then gunfire, and the critical moment was capped when an elderly Serbian grandmother was tossed to her death in an abandoned well.

In the space of two hours, bedlam raced through a two-block area. Fortunately, the hysteria didn't spread because police and citizens put a heavy-handed end to it. Afterwards, few, if any, wanted the destruction repaired.

Stephen Huey

It was a sure reminder of how easy it was for a society to lose control.

The UN Jeep stopped in front of a coffee bar where three small boys played near the entrance. Dressed in his black police uniform and a light blue UN beret, Burnwell looked imposing. So much so, before he and Davis reached the door, one of the boys rushed to open it, and all three gave a salute.

In the center of the bar sitting alone with a bottle of Rakija was the "local mafia" boss, Sasha Leskovac. He was a large man with dark hair and a thick beard. With the exception of the modern clothing, he looked like some Serbian Patriarch of old. His great size matched his approach to living, "bigger than life." Before Davis and Burnwell could join the boss, they were stopped at the entrance by a couple of Sasha's boys, who gave them a quick once over.

"Ah, Ms. Davis, you bring the John Wayne. Come join me."

Being waved over, the couple was allowed to pass and take a seat at Leskovac's small table. It seemed a waiter appeared out of nowhere, placed shot glasses in front of them, and filled each from the bottle. The three touched glasses in welcome.

"To, America," said the big Serb. "I like America, favorite. But you bomb my country tomorrow."

"It's not us; it's NATO."

"John Wayne; is there a difference?"

"How can you be so sure? Milosevic still has a window for compliance with NATO's demands."

"Ms. Davis, you don't know Slobodan. NATO should build a statue to him, their most willing enemy. But, it is the life, what can I do? I am just man from village. So, my friends, what brings you?"

"Who attacked us last night?"

"Someone who doesn't like you. John Wayne, you're too much the policeman, always you want black or white. Simple answers to complex questions. But sometimes, it is simple, very simple. When you're bombed, you run like a hell! Simple. Now, talking to you, how does this help man from village?"

Davis took a small black-covered edition of the King James Bible from inside Burnwell's map case and slid it over to Leskovac; an unusual gift for an Eastern Orthodox Christian. But when opened, he saw numerous $100 bills inside the pages. It was clear that everyone had the same belief.

"The Good Book," said Natalie while polishing off another perfectly rolled smoke.

"Yes," he replied and lit her cigarette. "I know who attacked, but it's not what you need. Most important, you must know who makes the puppets dance."

"Intelligence indicates Croatian paramilitary units organized the attack."

"Ms. Davis, Mihjilo wasn't attacked by a government. He was attacked by a greed. A greed of the single person; someone near to you."

"What does that mean?"

The Serbian boss let the question go unanswered. For the moment, the look in his eyes drifted to the past. "I was an officer in Yugoslav army. I was proud and my country, strong, that was long ago." He then leaned in close to his inquisitors and spoke in a low voice. "Go to Udvar.

Speak to my friend Zadro. He is border guard. He'll tell you what I mean." Sitting back, he eyed each of his visitors with a look to ensure they understood not only what he said, but also what he meant. Satisfied, the boss clapped his hands twice.

"Daj da čujem muziku!"
"Let me hear music!"

A familiar horn riff split the melancholy air, followed with a punch by the Godfather of Soul, *"I Got You."* Burnwell was out the door, but Natalie looked back in perplexity.

"A good Serb, this one," offered the strapping criminal boss and returned to his drink.

chapter

SIX

Zagreb, Croatia

All Croatian highways either started or ended in the ancient urban center along the Sava River, and for good reason. The pulse of the country emanated from this first century eastern European capital. Even during the worst times of the recent war, vendors in Zagreb's outdoor markets refused to yield. Daily, they hawked fruits and vegetables, mismatched athletic clothing, and truckloads of illegal CDs. The night was no different. Despite the scream of air raid sirens and Serbian rockets hitting the old city, young folks still hung out in parks and flocked at all hours to see the latest American movies.

A light snow had begun to fall as a white Peugeot 405 SRI rolled into the circular drive of the home belonging to Josip Mihjilo. In this slice of Zagreb, Gornji Grad, the eighteenth and nineteenth century townhouses dotting the boulevard were large ornate reminders of the Habsburg dynasty, imposing and cold. Longvue and Nakamura, with a small black leather backpack slung over her shoulder, exited the vehicle and went to the front door.

Parked two blocks away facing the home, a young man with close-cropped black hair spotted the couple and dialed his Nokia mobile phone.

"The policeman and girl are here. Yes, I will do this." He rang off and continued to watch.

Longvue tried the bell, but no one replied. Growing impatient waiting, as well as cold, he banged on the door hard with his fist. The force swung it open; still no living soul answered.

"*Zdravo. Zdravo*, hello, Mr. Mihjilo. Mr. Mihjilo, are you home sir?"

After they pushed the door open, Kazuko and Tyler stepped inside and promptly learned why no one had come to call. At the other end of a long corridor, seated and slumped across a desk, was the body of a person they presumed to be Josip Mihjilo. Moreover, the inside of the place was a wreck.

Getting to the son of the White Wolf was an indoor obstacle course. As they proceeded toward the victim, the couple had to weave their way through expensive tables, chairs, carpets, paintings, all pulled down, all torn apart, and all scattered.

The upper torso of the middle-aged Mihjilo was lying across the blood-splattered chestnut executive desktop with his head tilted to the right. Tyler observed a gunshot wound a little below the left ear and determined it must have come from a distance because the entry point was small and clean. The bullet entered through the base of his skull and exited the forehead, evidenced by the larger hole above the left eye. Stepping around the back of the body, Longvue saw that the dead man's right pant leg was soaked with blood from the knee to the cuff. A closer examination revealed the deceased had also been shot through the kneecap.

"Is this?" Kazuko started.

"Mihjilo, or what's left of him," said Longvue as he took two sets of rubber gloves from his jacket pocket and handed a pair to her.

"Where did you get these?"

"I'm a policeman, remember?"

Nakamura smirked and turned her attention to the whirlwind of devastation in the adjacent library. She donned her gloves and made her way carefully through the wreckage of the office toward the other room while Tyler conducted his investigation of the crime scene around the desk.

Picking up on the smeared trail of blood leading through to the adjoining room, she paused at the large pocket doors, pushed fully open, which separated the two stately expanses. A glow from the burning hearthside coupled with a single floor lamp threw long eerie shadows over the book-lined chamber. Still, the blood marks along with muddy footsteps could be seen easily. "What could they have possibly been looking for? They know I have the book," Kazuko said looking back at Tyler.

"Well, Agatha Christie, you seem sure it was more than one person who did this."

"Had to be; when we arrived, didn't you see the different footprints at the front door? The snow's been falling for only a short time. I thought you were the detective?"

"I am," said Longvue, slightly annoyed at missing such an obvious clue. After a few more minutes of inspecting the rifled desk, the dead man, and the area immediately around, the Texan concluded. "There's nothing else here I need." Joining his friend at the doorway, he clicked on the library's overhead lights and took in everything he saw. "Do me a favor and stay here while I look the room over."

Kazuko watched as the lean shamus stepped delicately and methodically around the setting gathering information. First, he inspected the French doors, which communicated to an outside courtyard garden. He then noted tracks from there to the well-worn black leather chair, where a pool of dark red blood at the foot and the base of the seat was still moist.

Next, Tyler thoroughly examined the bookshelves on either side of the fireplace and also the library ladder. Returning to the chair, he focused his attention on the tableside next to it. Taking a pen from his pocket, he poked through the full ashtray, separating and counting the extinguished cigarette butts. Finally, with a great deal of satisfaction painted on his face, he whistled his way back to his counterpart.

"You're in high spirits, Detective. Do you mind sharing what you've discovered?"

"Well, it's not much," Tyler started with false modesty, "but it's clear two suspects attacked our victim. They entered and exited through the French doors from the garden. One of our killers was tall, well over six feet, probably young, and likes Marlboros. The other appears to be of average height, much more experienced, and a chain smoker of State Express 555's.

"This violent episode started here at the chair, and it appears they questioned Mihjilo for some time, but he refused to answer. So, they shot him through the kneecap to loosen his lips. But that guy was just like his old man, one tough son-of-a-bitch; even in the shock of his unbelievable pain, he had the presence of mind to try and trick his attackers."

Tyler paused to light a smoke and perceived that his workman-like construction of events had impressed Ms. Nakamura, or so he thought. Delighted, he continued.

"Mihjilo told them what they were looking for was in the desk. So, the tall one drug the bleeding recalcitrant across the room while the other fella remained here. At the desk, Mihjilo went for that 9mm Croatian pistol, which is on the floor, unfired, near the wall. It was almost a fatal surprise for the big one, but his partner was able to nail Mihjilo before he could get off a shot. The two went back to their search, which I'm fairly sure was unsuccessful. And, as I said, they exited the same way they came in."

Taking another draw from his Marlboro light, Tyler exhaled in triumph and waited for the sure praise of his amazing deduction. But one doesn't always get what one wants.

Kazuko's smile changed to a giggle, then to outright laughter in a matter of moments. "Okay, Sherlock, I can see why you say there were two people. That's evident from the muddy footprints. But how do you know one is taller than the other? And for that matter, that the shorter one is a chain smoker?"

Skepticism of his observations was nothing new, and Longvue welcomed it. "It's right there in front of you. Clearly, the bookshelves on both sides of the fireplace have been ransacked. But only on the left side are there muddy footprints on top of the counter and library ladder. Also, these footprints match those near the black leather chair. On the right side of the fireplace the only footprints are the larger ones, and they're only to be found on the floor. Therefore, the man on the right hand side was tall enough to reach up and pull down all the books. Whereas the fella on the left needed the ladder."

"Okay, fine," Nakamura replied with some agitation in her voice, "but what about the chain smoking and one being younger and less experienced?"

"I said the tall man was probably young, but he definitely has less experience than the other man. The tall one drug Mihjilo over to the desk and nearly got killed because he wasn't paying attention. If you look on the floor near the desk you can see there are deep hard muddy marks in the carpet where he pushed his large feet down in an effort to run. Obviously, he was surprised when Josip

Mihjilo produced the gun, but his partner, not so much. The shorter man shot Mihjilo from across the room and hit him in the back of the head. Takes a cool hand to make that shot, and that only comes from experience. As for chain smoking, there are seven State Express 555 cigarette butts in the ashtray."

"How do you know it was the smaller man who was the chain smoker and not the other?"

"Because a big muddy footprint put out a Marlboro on the library carpet and that was the only Marlboro cigarette butt I found."

"Very good, very good," she said, in a tone that seemed both irked and impressed. "Wait a second, you said they didn't find what they were looking for; how do you know that, smart guy?"

"I said I was fairly sure. But consider the facts. They had to shoot Mihjilo in the kneecap to make him talk, and even then he tried to double-cross the bastards. No, I don't think he told them what they wanted to hear before they killed him."

"Well, you seem to have an answer for everything, Detective Longvue."

"Hardly. But I do know this is a crime scene we need to vacate."

Trying as best they could to follow their original footsteps, the two headed back to the front door.

"I must say you handle dead bodies pretty well."

"In school I spent summers with my uncle," she said.

"What does that mean? Your uncle was dead every summer?"

"Sort of. He's a mortician. His apartment is above the shop."

"Kazuko, that's creepy."

"Yeah, but like everything else, you get used to it. Although, there was this one time," Nakamura's voice trailed off.

"One time what?" asked Longvue, having almost made it back to the entrance. Getting no reply, he turned to see her frozen in place, eyeballing the carving atop the newel at the foot of the staircase. It was the figure of a woman cradling something in her arms. Then, as if possessed, Nakamura leaped onto the stairs, took the sculpture in hand, and pulled it, pushed it, and twisted it.

"What's got into you?"

"Tyler, it's Psyche!"

"You don't say."

"No, it has to be, Tyler, don't you see? This is the connection."

"Connection? Connection to what? That's just a statue of some woman holding a cheese box or something."

"No, it's a loaf of bread. She feeds it to Cerberus to enter and leave the underworld."

"Oh, right."

Finally, she gave up the struggle with the statuary because it wouldn't budge.

"Come on, Stickman, I need a hand; this has to be the answer."

"Kazuko, you've lost me. That statue is the answer to what?"

"The book; it all fits. The chance of coincidence is astronomical. Are you going to help me or what?"

Since it was obvious she was determined to have her way, Longvue walked over to the side of the staircase and tried moving the wooden sculpture; no luck.

"Look, this is one piece of wood," he said and slapped the statue. "It's not moving; solid as brick."

He kicked the base of the post to emphasize his pronouncement and they both heard an audible click. Looking down, a small portion of the staircase had popped ajar. Longvue opened it further with his foot and squatted down, looked inside, and pulled out a small hardback book wrapped in a clear airtight bag. On the book's cover was a picture of Raphael's Cupid and Psyche, which Nakamura recognized on the spot.

"May I see it?"

In an instant, she removed the wrapper and flipped through the tome. Thick with pages, each was filled with numbers and letters similar to the first book given to her by Old Mihjilo. But even with a short inspection, it was obvious to her this was some kind of formatting template that had been used extensively. Smudges from pencil entries marked and erased countless times in designated spaces were all throughout the book.

"What does this mean?"

"I'm not sure, Tyler, but this must be what they were looking for."

"Okay, put it in your bag. We gotta get out of here." She did so and the couple headed to the door.

Outside, the snow was coming down much heavier and in larger flakes. Longvue, on his cell, called UN HQ and gave a long and detailed report of what they had found. This went on for some time, and quite naturally,

Nakamura got bored. She strolled over to the car and it was there that her dullness found energy with the help of the fresh snowfall that had accumulated on the roof of the auto. It was a little wet from melting, which to her calculations, made it perfect.

"Yeah, that should do it. We'll wait here for the police. No, we're okay. There's no one else around. *Ciao*." Right after Tyler rang off, Nakamura's doldrums were cured.

Smacked with a slushy snowball, Longue felt cold streaks of wetness as it ran down the side of his neck. He turned, saw another ice ball in flight, and tried to duck, too late. Socked again, Kazuko had another palatable hit.

"One more strike and I get a turkey," she said with a giggle. "Oh, wait, I already have one." Smiling at her obscure bowling reference, the demure human rights worker prepared more ammunition for the coming brawl. Longvue obliged. Soon, they chased each other around the car slinging snowballs for attack and insults for poor marksmanship. But the fun was short-lived.

On either end of the narrow street leading to the house, the engines of two black Mercedes roared and sped their direction. Seeing they were cut off, Longvue grabbed Nakamura by the hand. "Let's go!"

In a dead run, the couple cut across the driveway to the rear of the house. As they rounded the back, the two black cars slammed into the white Peugeot and pinned it. Branagh and his young, tall, buzz-cut companion jumped out and gave chase.

From the back of the house there was a clear path to the city center and all that came with it. No matter the time of day or night, the streets of Zagreb's upper town were always packed with people and vehicles driving the engine of this eastern capital.

As quickly as they could, Longvue and Nakamura weaved their way in, around, and through the throng milling about the streets. Moments later Branagh and his partner did the same, but lost sight of their targets due to the goo-gob of shuffling proletariat and their motorcars. Unfortunately for the fleeing couple, their concealment was short-lived. When stopped at a corner by heavy passing traffic, Branagh, only two blocks away, saw them.

Finding a break in the jam of cars, Longvue and Nakamura zigzagged their way to a streetcar and made the running boards just before it left. Looking back, Tyler saw that their pursuers had boarded the tramcar just behind them.

Through the packed trolley, the UN comrades pushed their way to the front. As their tram moved slowly through an intersection turn, Longvue pushed the car doors open and shouted, "Jump!" With Nakamura by the hand and a torrent of Croatian expletives following them from the screaming streetcar attendant, they leaped from the slow moving car.

Outside, the festive snow shower had turned to a miserable snowstorm, making visibility poor and footing even worse. Landing on the street, Nakamura was able to keep her feet, but Longvue slid and fell on a patch of ice. He stood, but immediately slipped and dropped. He stood again; again the same. Nakamura came over to help and they were both down. Looking back, the couple saw the other cable car lumbering closer. Like two dogs, they scampered on all fours to unfrozen ground, made it to their feet, and sped across Nikola Šubic Zrinski Square to the Hotel Dubrovnik.

When the second streetcar arrived at the spot, the assassins jumped off as well. Amazingly, both landed standing, but dropped like bowling pins when they tried to run, up then down, up then down. This bit went on for a while until they figured out they had to crawl to get off the ice as well. Still, they were able to keep a bead on their targets and, when the gunmen did make it to their feet, they followed.

Rushing into the hotel, Longvue realized he and Nakamura were drawing attention, so they slowed to a fast walk. To their left was the crowded lobby bar of the Dubrovnik, open, large, and just what they needed. Quickly, they found their way to the back and searched for another exit.

Right behind them a rather bulky doorman entered, clapping his hands to shake off the cold. Taking off his heavy dark coat and red service hat, he laid them across the railing and walked away.

Next, the two assassins rushed in and scouted for their marks. Longvue was able to observe them by carefully using the ample pedestrian camouflage offered in the bar. What amazed him was how quickly the two killers blended with the surroundings, particularly Branagh. What Tyler didn't know was that blending was the Irish hit man's specialty.

Even with his long, red hair, Jason Branagh was the quintessential of ordinary. Not tall, not short, not fat, not thin, not ugly, not handsome; he was the kind of fellow one meets but forgets a moment later, which, in his line of work, was useful.

Stopping for a spell, Jason lit a smoke and did the same for his pal. Then the two strolled to the check-in desk opposite of the front door, all the while searching.

The problem for Longvue and Nakamura was the large chunk of open real estate between them, the killers, and the front door. Finding no back exit, the couple's options were thinning to nil until Tyler noticed the doorman's winter jacket and hat on the rail, which gave him an idea.

Ensuring to keep at least one person between him and his followers at the front desk, Longvue made his way to the rail and snatched the head cover and overcoat.

"Hello?"

Turning, Tyler found the distinctively British female voice belonging to the one thing he didn't need at that moment. He was eye to eye with an attractive flight attendant who had had a few too many glasses of wine and was ready to make a new friend.

"Hi," returned the Texan quickly as he tried to pass her by. Looking just over her shoulder, he saw Branagh and his associate making their way to the bar area.

"May I buy you a drink?" she said, taking him by the arm. In this situation, Tyler estimated he had two choices: refuse and chance a scene with an inebriated blonde calling attention to himself and her or; accept and chance a scene with an inebriated blonde calling attention to himself and her.

Quick on the mark, he shot back, "I'd love one, a tall gin and tonic if you can find it. Let me tell my friends and I'll join you at the bar." They each smiled and the pickled attendant, used to taking drink orders, went off to fill it.

Returning to Nakamura, he put on the coat, wrapped her up in the front part, donned the cap, and moved to the front exit at an angle, shielding their faces from the Irish killer and his companion. Amazingly, they made it to the door of the hotel and outside without incident or his drink.

"Što je to? To ne pripada vama."

"What is this? This doesn't belong to you."

Spinning, they found a short, plump, red-faced hotel concierge eyeing them warily from the bell stand at the entrance. Longvue took off the getup and put it across the hotel belvedere.

"Žao nam je prijatelj, ovdje idete."

"Sorry buddy, here you go."

Recognizing an American, the round one shifted to loud, broken English. "No, you are trying to steal coat and hat!"

"Sorry, sorry," Longvue offered apologetically, but was unable to stop his smile because the guy sounded like the cartoon character Boris Badenov from "The Rocky and Bullwinkle Show."

"No, Americans! You can not come and take as you want!" He grabbed Nakamura by the arm. "I call police."

With a swift right foot, the peace-loving human rights officer proved she was no pushover. Kazuko connected with a solid kick to the shin; still the corpulent Croatian was able to hang on. But after the next blow, he wasn't so lucky.

In police parlance it's called a brachial thump, and Longvue executed it perfectly. A hard fist strike where the neck meets the shoulder sent the fleshy front-door man to the ground.

"Wow," exclaimed Nakamura, "where did you learn that?"

"I keep telling you, I'm a policeman."

Tyler took her hand and they quickly ran away into the snowy night. A few moments later, two hotel employees rushed outside to aid the fallen one. More followed, and soon a crowd gathered out front of the Hotel Dubrovnik. Among the gaggle were Branagh, his tall partner, and Tyler's newest blonde friend; all three had missed their assignments.

chapter

SEVEN

Vukovar, UN Transitional Area: UN Medical Station

Despite a howling snowstorm that blew near white-out conditions, the well-lubricated driver of a 1994 Toyota pick-up weaved slowly along the road from one side to the other. Remarkably, the operator found and was able to guide the vehicle into the parking lot without running off into the ditch on either side of the entrance ramp. In further amazement, the truck whipped into a tight parking space, slipping past its parked neighbors by less than an inch on either side. One problem—the end of the space was piled high with snow.

Fortunately for all concerned, a header into the six-foot ice packed mound put an end to the circus ride and saved lives. Lights out, engine off, and out stumbled one pickled policeman, Mark Burnwell. With his crutches dragging, he snaked his way inside the UN Med Station.

Drinking alcohol of almost any amount was never a good mix for the Mormon. To his credit, firewater didn't make him offensive, but it didn't make him particularly graceful either, and at 245 pounds, goofy and clumsy wasn't good for the furniture.

All was quiet as Burnwell limped into the dark and vacant outer office of the emergency room. When he saw an empty gurney he set off in a ramble toward his bed for the night. But what he didn't see was a metal trashcan, which his right foot punted like a Pop Warner football across the linoleum floor. When it hit, the Grambling State Marching Band drum section couldn't have made more noise. Bumbling in a vain attempt to catch the errant container, he banged into the gurney and sent the wheeled contraption zipping across the room. When it crashed to a halt against a desk, it sent a metal file box loud and hard to ground.

Additionally, the sudden stop of the rolling bed caught Burnwell, who was in hot pursuit, by surprise. Leaping up, his momentum sent him over the getaway gurney, the desk, and onto the floor. Undaunted and de-termined, he made it to his feet and tried again. Latching onto the gurney, he flung himself on top of it, and once again the laws of physics took over and sent him gliding across the room in the other direction. This time the ride ended when his sled and the top of his coconut head nailed a six-drawer filing cabinet buttressed by the wall of the building. "Jeeeezzzuuss," he bellowed and rubbed his bald noggin. Fortunately, there was a blanket folded at his feet. Pulling it up without incident he turned to his side and the show was over, almost.

The commotion brought Dr. Margaret Lovejoy running. She flipped on the light and scanned the room. Quickly she spotted the culprit, a potted policeman prone on the palanquin.

"Comfortable?" she inquired.

"Your accommodations need some attention, Doc."

"Planning to stay the night, are we?" When she came within striking distance, the overpowering redolence of industrial strength Rakija assaulted her. "Oh, my word, you had better, dear."

"You know, we're, we're going to have to tell Mr. Truman. Uh, you know he's Mr. T, that just occurred to me," the big fella said and giggled like a silly teenager. "I pity the fool," this guffaw brought him to tears.

"Aren't we a clever policeman. Get some sleep."

"No, no, wait. We're going to need new guar ... guards at Udvar border. When the bombing started, all the Serbs left, gone ... skeeeeeedaddled."

"And you had a busman's holiday, too," Margaret answered in an annoyed and amused voice. "My, we did have a grand time tonight. And what were you doing up at the border?"

"Oh Maggie, Maggie, Maggie finding out what I knew ... I knew to be true and hearing more lies. The border guys said this Irish guy and some American or, something like an American, came through ... through. Probably, Canadian, I don't know, could have been a man or, uhm."

"A woman?"

"That's it: right, Doc," he said and touched his nose in a theatrical fashion. "I don't know that either. But these folks are bad business, these two ... assassins."

Burnwell propped up on one arm and turned his bloodshot glazed eyeballs toward her.

"Gets better. They said the American or Canadian was really a Russian Colonel." His arm slipped and he fell laughing.

"New world order, Doc. Swear to God, they're taking over."

There was no answer. He waited a moment longer, then the lights went out, and Col. Dr. Margaret Emma Lovejoy was long gone.

"Doc? Uh, Doc? Guess my work is done," the big Mormon asserted with great satisfaction and went to sleep.

A lone United Nations Volkswagen bus motored along the "Road of Brotherhood and Unity." Opened in 1950, the Brotherhood and Unity Highway was still the major artery between Zagreb in the west and Belgrade in the east, but it represented so much more than a mere road.

The divided super-highway served as an enduring allegory to Tito's relentless effort to unite the country long split between the eastern Serbs, the western Croats, and the Muslims in the middle. And in a larger sense, like Tito himself, once Brotherhood and Unity was built, the route defied convention and went its own way.

Despite the deadly divide of the Cold War, pitting Eastern Steel against Western Gold, the world was free on this road. For more than forty years, almost anyone from anywhere could travel through communist Yugoslavia using this well constructed, well-maintained highway. And so, they did. NATO allies, Warsaw Pact communists, even the French, drove from Austria to Greece and back again along what the locals called the 'Autoput.' But when Yugoslavia self-destructed, the brutal war and chronic neglect put an end to that. Where once the thruway teemed with commercial and personal traffic, now hours passed before a stray vehicle went along the Autoput in either direction. On this night, the Volkswagen bus hadn't encountered a single soul since leaving Zagreb.

It was long after midnight. The snow had stopped falling around 10:45 and the sky had been clearing since. Luckily, Longvue and Nakamura had been able to flag down the UN bus near the Zagreb city center and hitch a ride. Piloted by a young Russian soldier, it just so happened that he and the Volkswagen were headed back to Osijek.

Tyler was up front with the Russian and Kazuko was in the back, working. She had a flashlight out and was comparing Young Mihjilo's book to a stack of papers, which was a copy of Old Mihjilo's book. As a precaution, Nakamura had copied a large portion of the old man's book and hid it before contacting Tyler. She might be new at this game but it appeared she learned quickly.

"Хорошо, что вы пришли вместе, мы мерзли,"

"It's good that you came along, we were freezing," Longvue said as he lit cigarettes for them both.

With a grin, the soldier replied,

"Также хорошо для меня, я был потерян."

"It's also good for me. I was lost."

Reaching into a compartment on the door, the young man produced a bottle,

"Это согреет вас."

"This will warm you."

"Спасибо,"

"Thanks," returned Tyler and quickly knocked back a big swallow. Just as quickly he broke into a harsh hacking cough.

"Черт! Вы могли бы летать на самолете с этим,"

"Damn! You could fly a plane with this," he said gasping with tears.

"Мы делаем*!"*

"We do," said the Russian proudly.

Working hard to refocus from being walloped by Belarus booze, Longvue looked back on his industrious friend. Still locked into her task, as she had been for over two hours, she was writing down numbers, counting letters, putting things backwards, shifting things up, then down, and so on and so on. Taking the moonshine with him, Longvue moved between the seats and sat next to her.

"Here, try some of this; it'll warm you up."

"Thanks."

"Careful it's ... " Tyler's effort to stop her was too late. Before he finished the sentence she had thrown down a gulp, handed the bottle back, and continued on with her work.

"Okay, then," said he, impressed and bewildered.

"At times I think I have a thread, but it quickly unravels. It's a substitution code, but I just can't seem ... " She trailed off as she looked up and found the perplexed policeman staring at her. "Why are you looking at me that way, Tyler?"

"It's just, weird. I mean, swigging hooch like a cowboy is one thing, but you're a code breaker, too?"

"I'm a woman of parts," she exclaimed, but her glib remark fell flat, so she tried again.

"I started doing these puzzles when I was a young girl. My father broke code during the war. He also loved Glenfiddich. I picked up the passion for both."

"The war?" asked Longvue, "Which one?"

"For my father, there was only one, World War II. A time when being a Japanese American didn't make one a lot of friends."

"I'll bet. Was he put in one of those camps?"

"Worse; he joined the Army. He didn't talk about it much but he loved his work. He was a linguist. And even though he spoke fluent Japanese, what did the Army do? They sent him to Europe."

"Yeah, the Army makes life a lot of fun that way. I was in for about a decade," ruminated the lean Texan extinguishing his smoke in the overstuffed ashtray. "Didn't make it for my full twenty though. There was just no way I could stand ten more years of that much fun." Leaning back and stretching his legs, Tyler clasped together his hands on his chest and asked, "So, he taught you a few tricks?"

"Yeah, it was a game we all played: 'crack the code for cash.' What he'd do is write out different ciphers and put a price on them, some easy, some hard, some bulletproof. Of course, the harder the code, the more it was worth; it was just a few bucks. But I was better at it than my brothers. And my father took great delight in that. We all had such a wonderful time, I wish I could … " She trailed off as tears welled. She wiped her eyes with the sleeve of her coat, took a breath, and finished her thoughts. "He died two years ago; have you another cigarette?"

Tyler obliged and lit it. "Why not get some rest? Start fresh in a few hours."

"I think you're right."

She put the codebook and papers into her leather back pack and snapped off the flashlight. Inside, all went inky black, except for the tips of two glowing gaspers and the muted orange/yellow lights from the dashboard. Outside, the attention of both was drawn to night's wintertide vista.

With the clouds gone the big moon commanded the sky, throwing dark shadows from towering mountains onto the white valley floor. Dotted by warm and soft yellow lights from several small farmhouses, the view touched on the spiritual. Serenity. Beauty. It was Yugoslavia.

"Where's your home Tyler?"

"Houston, if I go back."

"Do you have family there?"

"No, I had a wife, but we split up four years ago."

"I'm sorry."

"Oh, don't be; it's better for both of us."

"If you don't mind me asking, what happened?"

"Greed. I knew Alice was selfish when I married her, or so I thought until Wednesday June 15, 1994."

"Could you be a little more exact?"

"Sure, that was the day Alice Paige Bellefontaine Longvue won the lottery, two million. Well, one and some change after taxes."

"This is a joke," said Kazuko rolling her eyes.

"No, I'm serious and it gets better. I didn't know she had won until I got this drunk phone call from her sister, Peggy, about a month later. As it turns out these two geniuses hatched a plan to skip off to the Caymans. But bless her heart, Alice Paige was true to form; she cut Peggy out at the last moment and literally left her at the airport. Alice is a real piece of work."

Longvue snatched up the bottle and took a more measured sip of the jet fuel, but still coughed a bit. He handed it to Kazuko and, of course, she downed it like water.

"Anyway, after the divorce I hired a financial advisor and started trying things. I joined and quit the police department, twice; owned a telephone book."

"Telephone book; one can own those things?"

"Not only that, Ms. Nakamura, one can make a good deal of money, but the work is mind-numbing, so I got rid of it; then a friend told me about this mission. Thought I'd give the old country a try since it's my mother's homeland and I can stumble through the language."

Nakamura gave him a blank stare, then a giggle that wouldn't stop. "Let me make sure I understand; you're a rich ex-cop who speaks fluent Serbo-Croat, as well as Russian, from what I just heard, and you call me weird? Tyler, either you're the luckiest man alive or ... "

"Or I'm a big fat liar? Yeah." He turned his gaze back out the window. "I get a lot of that."

"I'm sorry, but your story, it's, fantastic."

"I know," he said and locked his eyes with hers. "That's why I only tell it to people I really like."

Then it happened. It wasn't particularly graceful, but falling for someone normally isn't. According to the Oxford English Dictionary, there are about 171,476 words currently being used in the language, but at the moment neither of them could find a single one. Tyler took another drink, hacked out a cough like a TB patient, and fumbled the conversation forward.

"Uhm, so, your mom, what is it she does?"

Kazuko was in a situation she dreaded. Though her feelings for Mr. Longvue were the same, she wasn't especially keen on displaying them. It wasn't because she didn't want to; it was because she felt she didn't know how. Even the tears for her father a moment ago came with awkwardness. And, to make it worse, this inability to express her emotions also fed a Japanese stereotype she loathed, coldheartedness. But nature and culture don't let go easily. So, like many times before, she simply ignored it and moved on.

"Yeah, she's in New York; still a nurse and still with the UN. It's the family business, medicine, and the United Nations. It was my one and only path."

"That didn't sound too convincing. What other *path* would you have followed?"

"Pro golfer."

"Really? I didn't know you played golf."

"I don't, I'd have to learn, I suppose. But it's worth it for the outfits."

"Cute. Any other surprises, Ms. Nakamura?

"Actually, it's Mrs. Well, technically anyway. I haven't seen my husband in two, almost three years."

"Really?" Tyler replied. She studied his face and knew the surprise was genuine.

"I guess I should have said something before now but the time never seemed to be right. And it's something that doesn't come up easily in conversation. I mean one doesn't say, 'pass the butter please and I no longer live with my husband in case you're wondering.'"

"So, is this just a separation?"

"No, we're split for good. I just haven't got around to making it final."

"Does he want the break up?"

"At first he didn't, but that changed." She took a deep pull from her Marlboro and forged ahead. "I met David in college and we married just before graduation. Seemed like the right thing to do. All of our friends were getting married, our parents loved the match, and David and I, well, we really liked each other, but."

"But now you see it wasn't your decision to do so. You two married because everyone else wanted you to," said Longvue.

"You're quick to understand."

"Yeah, I've been through this with a fat bald man."

"You married a fat bald man, Tyler?"

"Well, Mark Burnwell and I are close but, no. We had a similar conversation though, and Mark said decisions work best when made by the people affected."

"Obviously."

"Yeah, Kazuko, that's what I said, too. But I gave it some thought, doesn't always work that way, does it?"

"No, I guess not." She tapped out the cigarette and looked through the window at the quiet passing scenery. "Are you really as boring as Mark says you are?"

His hand touched her shoulder. "How am I doing so far?"

When her wide-eyes met his, her emotional rollercoaster started again. *I don't know if I can do this*, she thought. Tyler saw her hesitancy but he took the chance. They kissed. Then they kissed again.

In the pale light of the night sky, the Volkswagen bus continued alone on the highway. All around the full moon's soft touch blended the world into a singular moment; shimmering white from snow-covered fields, dots of twinkling yellow light from far-off villages, and ghostly blue shade from distant dark mountains.

chapter

EIGHT

Osijek, Croatia

The dull gray light of a winter morning seeped into Stephen Truman's twelfth story penthouse atop the Hotel Osijek. It was Sunday, early, and tranquil, so naturally, the phone rang. Jolted awake, the UN Chief opened one eye, hoping it was a dream. It rang again.

"Damn it." Staying prone, Stephen reached over, took the receiver, and slid it next to his ear. "Yes?"

"We need to talk as soon as possible," came the excited and concerned voice of Margaret Lovejoy.

Silence.

"Stephen, are you there?"

Cradling the phone between his ear and the pillow, he tried to read his wristwatch.

"Yes, yes. My plane from Zagreb ran late, we arrived only a few hours ago. What do you need?"

From his left side came the slender arm of Claire Anjou crossing his shoulders as she adjusted herself next to him.

"We can't speak about this over the phone, but what I have to say is most urgent. May I come round to your accommodation?"

Removing the Anjou appendage, he sat up on the side of the bed, rubbed his face, and tried, again, to focus on his Vostok Komandirskjie timepiece. It was a big ugly hunk of metal, springs, and gears stamped with the official ЗАКАЗ МО СССР, by Order of the Ministry of Defense of the USSR. It was a gift from Zavisha, which appropriately epitomized the communist mentality. Like so many things from that regime, instead of it being designed to suit the user, it was built and the user was strapped on. Still, as hideous as it was, it kept excellent time.

"No, no, if we must, I'll meet you at my office. Make it an hour and a half."

Replacing the phone to its cradle, Stephen sat with eyes closed and tried desperately to think of a way to get out of what he'd just agreed to do. Dashing off to his office to meet with the energized English doctor wasn't a particularly promising start to a Sunday, nor any other day for that matter. *Her voice sounded out of character*, he thought. *But if the normally stoic Maggie Lovejoy was cranked-up, it's a good bet that something evil was on the way.*

"Who are you meeting?" queried a slumberous Anjou.

"Margaret."

"You get around, counselor," Claire said, with neither opening an eye nor questioning him further. It was all understood. In this, their stolen moment, convention was set aside. Both were married, to other people, and both knew the relationship would not/could not last. So, for the last few months, their world centered on the here and now, going on with their lives with neither preamble nor postmortem. But even that arrangement couldn't escape an inconvenient truth, age.

Two irreparable dilemmas beset Summer/Winter relationships, energy and references. When Claire said 'let's go out, stay up, or have a run,' Stephen said 'let's stay home, get some sleep, or run only if chased.' Then, there were the stories.

Initially, hearing the tales of Stephen's life was part of what brought them together. His career was a tapestry of interesting, harrowing, and often comical threads told from the elevated position of an actor in global affairs. But with the two having such uneven stations, the information usually flowed in one direction. Predictably, as time went on, she grew weary of hearing yet another story. Stephen R. A. Truman was keenly aware this was a time out of season. But he had determined to have it both ways, like so many other things in his life.

Born in Northern Rhodesia, Stephen Roosevelt Adolf Truman was cautiously but famously named for leaders on both sides of the global war. It was 1943 and the outcome was too close to call. His parents wanted to make sure he was on the winning side of the fight no matter the conclusion. This was a tactic he'd employed throughout his life and with considerable success, so far. He stood and made his way to the bathroom.

Vukovar, UN Transitional Area: UN Medical Station

Flat on his back and still on the gurney, Burnwell snored loudly dead to the day, maybe the decade. By following the cacophony, Natalie Davis walked into the room and found her policeman. She studied the lawman, then smiled mischievously and twisted the big fella's nose. Awoke with a start, Burnwell jumped up and she jumped back.

"Good morning, doll-face."

Rubbing his aching snout, which was the least of his ills, Burnwell grunted, dropped, and rolled back to his side. But the determined Texan had other plans for the trashed Mormon. In a loud and purposely irritating voice she asked, "Did you gain anything from your visit to the border?"

"A hangover."

"Anything else?"

"Do we have to do this now?" he said with a face that showed the jackhammers working in his head.

"Oh my, yes, while it's still fresh in your pea brain."

"Look, Natalie, give me an hour. Then I'll tell you the wild-ass stories I heard about the Russians, the CIA, hell, who shot Kennedy, everything."

"Nothing doing, big boy. This sounds fascinating! And you can tell me all about it at breakfast. Come on we're headed to Osijek."

She took Mark by the arm and pulled him upright, "Okie dokie, big fella. Up, Simba, up."

Vukovar: UNTAES Headquarters

Unlike military operations, peacekeepers got weekends off. As Margaret Lovejoy hurried down the empty dark hallway at HQ, the only light she saw burning was coming through the open door of Stephen Truman's office. Once inside, she launched into her dire report, "Stephen, I've learned some most disturbing news. Last night ... "

After making her way to the middle of the room, she stopped as suddenly as she had started when spotting Charles Baxter in the corner.

"Oh, I'm sorry to interrupt; I didn't know you were busy."

"That's quite all right, Margaret," said Truman, seated at his desk with a concerned and puzzled face. "Now what is your news?"

Her pause had become as awkward as her gaze, which was fixed upon the short State Department officer. She turned away and, with a completely blank expression, said, "There is going to be a mass demonstration today in front of HQ. It concerns the bombing in Kosovo."

"Yes, Margaret, we know."

"Colonel, would you care for some tea?"

"No, thank you, Charles."

Then, for the next thirty seconds, the three colleagues simply looked at each other like cows in a field. Finally, Stephen broke the silence.

"Margaret, do you have something more?"

"No, no. I didn't know you were aware of the situation. It's going to be an extremely large event from all reports, and with you in Zagreb for the last few days, I wanted to make sure."

With that, and a klutzy sort of wave, the bumbling episode ended with Lovejoy's exit.

"How extraordinary," remarked Truman.

"What's that?" snorted Baxter.

"Margaret, just now; she wouldn't talk on the phone, insisted on meeting me here, then, well, you heard it. At times I find the woman inscrutable."

"There you have it, Stephen. She's a woman."

"Thank you, Charles. Yes, humph, seems a morning for perplexity; first Margaret's mysterious energy, and now your news."

"Your confusion with Margaret, I understand, but there should be no confusion about Mr. Zavisha. Unless you're saying you never suspected him of being connected with Mihjilo's death."

"Charles, suspicion is what it is; I want to know the evidence against him."

"There's nothing rock solid yet. Proof is hard to obtain against this guy. There's a reason why he rose so quickly in the KGB, Stephen, and it wasn't because of his good looks."

"It appears I'm in your hands, Charles; so, what do you suggest?"

"Right now, nothing. Tea?"

chapter

NINE

Osijek, Croatia

Clouds had broken, and morning in the ancient eastern city of Osijek had become clear, cold, and crisp. Located on the banks of the Drava River since the Neolithic times, its name originated from the Croatian word meaning *ebb tide*. During the war, it sustained only moderate damage unlike its neighbor less than twenty miles away. As cruel fate determined, the horrors of the armed conflict flowed away from Osijek and smashed Vukovar. Perhaps there was power in a name.

Longvue and Nakamura were having coffee in a bakery near the city center. They had chosen the location because it offered an outstanding tactical view of both her apartment and the railroad station. But that's where their common effort ended. As soon as they were seated, the Japanese code breaker went one way while the pragmatic Texan went the other.

Nakamura was in the theoretical world, steadily working with the codebook trying to find a thread, a hint, a line of reason into the amazing labyrinth. Longvue, on the other hand, had both feet grounded in the applied. He tapped a locker key on the table and considered the situation; a plan of action, a fallback plan, a fallback to the fallback. Suddenly, their individual worlds aligned and struck. It was time to move.

"Locker 214, right?"

His words met dead air; she wasn't there.

"Kazuko, the locker number, 214?

"What? Oh, yeah, right."

"You know, this is classic life imitating art, stashing the book in a train station locker. It's like something out of *Mission Impossible*.

"It's not that bad," she countered, lighting a cigarette. "Moreover, I had to; if they had caught me with it, hell, I was cooked."

Tyler was learning and appreciating the fact that his partner was far from ordinary. She was brainy, there was no doubt about that, but it was in a blue-collar sort of way. As incredible as it seemed, it was just as easy to picture her answering questions about Plato's Republic on television's

Jeopardy as it was to see her rotating tires on a Malibu Classic. He lit a smoke and put on his hat and coat.

"Okay, I'm going to head over. Now, you stay here. But if I'm not back in ten minutes, or if you see trouble, I want you to disappear and call Burnwell."

"Got it," she said without looking up. He stood and leaned over her, but the best he could get was an I'm-busy-kiss, so he headed out the door.

After he left she looked up and watched her friend, but her mind was still far away. "And return to the mother," Nakamura said aloud. "In death, return to the mother. Return to the, return to the mother."

Epiphany!

Her eyes grew wide with excitement. After so many hours there was finally a chink in the wall that sealed the mysteries of the books.

"Oh, it couldn't be that simple. In death, the one is now three as they return to their mother. Return to the mother, that's it, yes, I think it works. Damn it, I need to go to my apartment."

Through the bakery window she saw Longvue on his way to the railway station. He had told her to stay put for safety, but her new thought was too important, too exciting to wait on his return. *Besides*, she thought, *my place is only across the road. A quick in and out and Bob's your uncle.* Gathering her things, she hurried to the entrance. Pausing at the door, she looked up and down the street. Seeing no one, especially Tyler, she flew.

Nothing prepares one for the disturbing sight of one's home after its been ransacked and pillaged. It's a stark and unsettling manifestation that somebody has gone through your personal belongings that makes one feel exposed and vulnerable. When Nakamura opened the door to her place, the salmagundi thumped her on the noodle.

"Jesus Christ," she exclaimed, almost afraid to enter, but the drive for her discovery pushed her forward. She slammed the door shut behind her and went to work hunting through the shambles of what remained of her apartment.

It seemed every book she owned was torn to shreds and laying on the floor. Luckily though, her prize had been spared. Under a pile of clothes and furniture she finally put her hands on Philip Mayerson's *Classical Mythology*. Flipping through to the index, she found her topic, "Death, mother of death." Turning to the page indicated, she read aloud, "To the West, to the West! Night is the mother of death and lives west across the sea. This has to be the key to it all."

Stunned by the revelation, she read the words again and again, in a sort of celebratory manner. Unfortunately, the observance had to be short-lived. She knew there was no time to waste. To make this gamble pay, she had to get back to Tyler to share her discovery. Quickly, she shoved the tome into her backpack and was away as promptly as she had arrived.

At the top of the stairway, just outside her Soviet era dump, Nakamura saw Longvue leaving the train station with the brown leather map case containing the book. Waving to him gleefully, she hurried down the steps. It was the discovery of a lifetime, and only two blocks separated her from sharing it with the world.

"Tyler, I have it," she said, almost screaming. Tyler had neither heard nor saw her as she tried to attract his gaze. She was supposed to be waiting in the bakery and that's where his attention and direction were fixed.

"Tyler, Tyler," she continued, but realized her pocket-sized voice wouldn't cover the distance to his ears. To the New Yorker in her, this wasn't going to be a problem for long.

Catching a cab at Eighth Avenue and West 33rd took something loud, like jet engine loud. A whistle at 120 decibels did the trick. So, the petite Human Rights worker stuck two fingers between her lips and punched it out. Needless to say, it nabbed the attention of the thin Texan.

At first sight, Longvue was livid seeing Nakamura away from the safety of the bakery. She had done exactly what he told her not to do, go to her apartment, classic. Yet, the sight of the animated, bundled-up, little Japanese woman jumping around like an Ewok on parade was just too goofy not to bring a smile to a frustrated face. However, reality quickly changed that.

A 1989 black Mercedes 300 screeched to a halt next to Kazuko. In the work of an instant, Branagh got out, swiftly took her by the arm, and pulled the fighting Ewok inside the car.

"No, no, you bastards," Longvue shouted in rage and took off in a mad futile run toward the fleeing sedan.

***

Driving a thoroughly hung-over Burnwell along the war-damaged road leading into Osijek had been great fun for Natalie Davis. Their white Jeep Cherokee bumped to a halt at a stoplight near the city center. Leaning out the passenger side window, with his head buried on his arms, was Burnwell in unrestricted misery.

"You didn't miss a pothole, did you?"

"Nope, doll-face, think I got them all."

"Nice work," muttered the big man.

Just as the light changed, Longvue zipped past the front of their Jeep. Davis leaned across Burnwell's back and demonstrated why she was one of the top Yell Leaders at Texas A&M.

"Tyler! Tyler, over here!"

The full lung whoop stopped Longvue dead in his tracks. He turned and ran back to their car with no hesitation. The skull-splitting projection of Davis' voice had also stopped Burnwell from any chance of recovery.

Swinging open the door, Tyler dove into the back seat while shouting, "They're taking Kazuko! Her apartment, go, go! There! There they are, the black Mercedes." Davis gunned the Magnum V-8 engine, wheels screeched in a scorched cloud of seared rubber, and Burnwell looked as if his world was about to end.

Davis' Jeep Cherokee blew the next two stoplights and was almost hit twice. Swerving in and out of traffic and pedestrians, she was gaining on Branagh's black Mercedes at breakneck speeds.

In the distance, the loud bells at the railway crossing had started to clang as the long wooden crossing arms began their slow descent to barricading the roadway. Street traffic travel had begun to stack up as cars stopped for the approaching train.

Branagh's Mercedes was forced to a sudden stop, caught in the waiting line of cars. Then, whipping to the wrong side of the street, his black sedan headed full tilt toward the crossing locomotive. Davis did likewise to keep up the pursuit.

Inside the Jeep, it appeared Burnwell's misery had coupled with the situation. His speech became strange and he seemed to embrace it. "We're on the wrong side of a two-way street, speeding toward an oncoming train." Then Mark flinched because a bullet ricocheted off the hood. "And they're shooting at us. What could possibly go wrong?"

By this time, the lumbering engine had entered the crossing, but neither the black Mercedes nor the white Jeep slowed. With the runaway black car speeding toward sure oblivion, Davis, Burnwell, and Longvue could do nothing more than watch.

The train whistle was now a constant. Even though it was moving slow, the weight of an average freight train requires more than a mile for it to come to a stop. Leaning out the cab window, the engineer tried to wave off the approaching automobiles. In spite of this effort, the Mercedes sped up.

"They can't make it," Tyler started, dumbfounded by the approaching calamity. "They can't!"

The pair of wooden crossing arms bounced to a rest upon the ground as Branagh's car hit the point of no return. Swinging slightly left, then right, for his Mercedes to gain precious space, the train and the black vehicle had arrived at their destiny.

Bursting through the crossing arms, the vehicle went airborne and flew across the tracks right in front of the locomotive. By the miracle of inches, they missed each other and gave certain death an IOU. Hitting the road in one piece, Branagh's black Mercedes rocketed off.

"I'll be damned," belted Davis as she hit the brakes and sent the Jeep skidding off the road. The white Cherokee came to rest in a ditch not four feet from the passing train. The three bailed out and dashed to the crossing. Between the slow passing freight cars, they saw Branagh's black vehicle speeding away north toward Beli Manastir. While they watched it disappear into the distance, there came a sound that never meant anything good.

Metal being ripped apart slowly isn't something one hears everyday, so it attained full attention. Turning toward their ride, the group witnessed the edge of an oversized railroad car split Davis' Jeep from front to rear with the ease of a hatchet passing through Jello.

Taking a seat on a nearby park bench, Davis rolled a cigarette and blurted the only word she could muster, "crap."

"Call for a wrecker," a disheartened Longvue mumbled as he walked off toward the city. "I'll get us some coffee."

He had to get away, he had to have time; the recrimination had already started. *Why didn't she just stay? Hell, why didn't I take her with me?* His frustration and anger were so great his body shook. With each step his pace quickened almost, breaking into a dash.

"What the hell was I thinking?" screamed Tyler to a world that gave no answers. Stopping, he looked around. He needed something, anything, to fill this void. He took off in a dead run toward the city.

After Longvue vanished into the throng, Burnwell dropped like a sack of potatoes next to Natalie, threw the fur-lined coat hood over his head, and fell back flat on the bench.

Sketching from several black and white photos taken a few days ago, Baxter outlined the shape of Vukovar's train station. The once quaint 150-year-old structure was severely damaged during the civil war. Yet, after four years of peace, it remained so. To the Serbs in the region, it was a stark reminder that they had lost the war. To the Croats, it was a manifest reminder that they had lost the peace.

A couple of years ago, Croatian President Franjo Tudjman thought it would be an excellent whistle stop on his "Train of Peace" tour. But neither Tudjman nor the rest of his cronies fully understood the negative symbolism that would be attached to the stunt, and the results were disastrous.

When the Croatian President's sleek modern train rolled into the shot-up, broken-down Vukovar station, it didn't make the Serbians feel as if hope had arrived; in fact, it was just the opposite. The Croats had won and now the Serbs felt they were getting their noses rubbed in it. So, as soon as Tudjman's train was in range, the large crowd at the station unleashed a ceaseless barrage of stones. The peace train didn't stop and neither did the hatred.

Next to Baxter was a newspaper that screamed in large bold type: *NATO Planes Bomb Kosovo.* As the Old Balkan hand took a break from his drawing, he scanned the *Daily,* then threw it down in disgust and scoffed, "Damn propaganda."

His cell phone rang.

"Baxter."

"Charles, it's Natalie. I found Longvue. He's safe, but Nakamura's been kidnapped."

"Always with the good news. Any details?" Outside, Baxter heard shouts and whistles that steadily grew in volume and number. He went to the window and saw what was left of the Serb community had descended on the front of the UN compound in another of their many protests. *This time it was about Kosovo,* he thought, *next week, who knows? There was plenty of misery.*

"Longvue told me two men forced Nakamura into a black Mercedes earlier."

Paying only half attention to her, Baxter asked, "Are you alone?"

"No, Burnwell and Longvue are with me."

"You three couldn't stop them?"

"We tried, but, no."

"Nakamura's gone. Nice work, Natalie. Considering our track record with the Mihjilo boys, she's probably safer."

"We'll contact the police. Maybe we can get a lead on the car."

"And maybe Milosevic is really a swell guy, just misunderstood," Baxter mumbled to himself in vexation as he looked at the newspaper again.

"Sir?"

"Nothing," said he and turned his attention back outside to the crowd.

"What's the noise in the background?" Davis queried.

"It's a cabaret. The Serbs are celebrating NATO bombing their homes. Call me with some good news. I could use it."

Davis rang off and Baxter put the phone into his pocket. His attention again went back outside and his thoughts drifted to what his thirty years in the Balkans had accomplished.

"We asked you to trust us," he said in a voice of resignation to the situation as it had played out. "We said we're going to take care of you. Then we bomb your relatives. Yeah, our policy in Yugoslavia makes perfect sense."

chapter

TEN

Osijek, Croatia

After a half-mile at a dead run, the overwhelming feelings of anger, frustration, and hate boiled down to a single driving force inside Tyler Longvue, revenge. Physical exertion clears the mind like nothing else.

Walking back from the city center, Longvue observed a UN Wrecker recovering what was left of their mangled ride. In one hand he had his mobile phone pressed against his ear and in the other he carried a small cardboard tray filled with three cups of strong black coffee and two clumps of Burek.

This lard-soaked staple of fried flaky dough filled with warm gooey cheese, Burek, could be found almost anywhere in the Balkans. Its name was the combination of two Slavic words: "Bu," meaning grease and "rek" meaning more grease.

"There's no time to argue about this, Nikita," the Texan insisted. "Honest to God, it sounds like you're more concerned about the books than her. All we know is that they left Osijek headed toward Beli Manastir. When I find out more I'll let you know." Longvue snapped his phone shut.

Upon his return, the thin man found his friends exactly where he'd left them. The only change was that Burnwell was now upright. A positive sign for someone with an All State hangover, but the wayward Mormon kept his head in his hands and didn't look up. Natalie reached over and took a coffee off the tray, while Longvue contemplated a way to get some kind of reaction from his ailing buddy.

Tearing off a chuck of the warm Burek, Tyler slowly waved it inches from the big fella's buried face. "Here, eat this."

"Eat me, Longvue."

Mark wasn't bouncing back too terribly fast, but the same wasn't the story concerning their Jeep. Amazingly, the vehicle recovery went without a hitch. In fact, the damaged Jeep was cleared away and a new one was ready to be issued in what amounted to record time. All that was left to be done was to sign the paperwork for the new ride and the three would be on their way. But the wheels of efficiency soon fell off when the vehicle receipt showed up on the neatly ordered clipboard carried by the petulant Capt. Lodvor Olsen.

When Tyler spotted Lodvor marching his direction in perfect military cadence, 30-inch steps at 120 steps per minute, he knew two things; first, signing for the Jeep was going to be a monumental pain-in-the-ass; and second, Capt. Olsen didn't like cigarette smoke. There was little he could do about the former, but for the latter, he lit up. Picking up her cue from Longvue, Natalie did the same.

Looking up as the pushy little captain arrived, Burnwell started, "Lodvor, my boy, always good to see you."

"Save your comical routine, Burnwell. This will cost you, all three of you."

"Ah, hell, Lodvor, this could have happened to anyone."

"No, not just anyone. You, Ms. Davis, and the other Texas cowboy there, only you two would challenge a train."

"Okay, no more trains. From now on just the small stuff, buses, and trucks." The strict captain wasn't amused by the comment, but in fairness Burnwell wasn't really trying.

"Enough jokes. You three will sign this paper, take full responsibility for the destroyed vehicle, and it will be deducted from your pay. It's been decided, and there will be no more questions concerning the matter."

In a flash, the pronouncements of this nepotistic Norwegian nabob had rekindled all Tyler's feelings of anger, frustration, and hate. To his credit, Longvue took a moment, expelled a long breath of smoke in the direction of the captain, then launched into a full-throated rebuke.

"What the hell do you mean, no questions? You have no idea what's going on or what's at stake. Jesus Christ, Lodvor, Kazuko's been kidnapped! But all you're concerned with is this frickin Jeep! Where the hell is your head? We've got to get out there!"

"Okay, Tyler you've made your point," broke in the calm but firm voice of Mark Burnwell. "My head isn't going to get any better with you shouting, Stickman. Now, let's take a moment and think about this."

Burnwell as a peacemaker wasn't a role any of the others recognized, which was evident from their sudden silence.

"You know, Lodvor, I give you a lot of crap. But there's one thing that I've always known to ring true. When you're right, you're right."

"What are you talking about? We're trying to save a life and all he wants to do is balance some imaginary checkbook."

"Look, Longvue, I understand. But it's not imaginary; this man has a job to do, and it ain't easy. I respect that about him. So, let's just get it over with." Turning back to the captain, Burnwell extended his hand for the clipboard. "We'll take full responsibility. Where do we sign?"

The blank expression on Lodvor Olsen's face was a clear indication he couldn't believe what he was hearing. He was giving orders, his words carried weight, and his commands were being followed. The young captain stood like a duck thumped upon the head, flummoxed.

Reaching out, Mark took the clipboard with its neatly typed sheets and signed each page without hesitation. When finished, he handed it to his bewildered and skeptical partner. After Tyler looked it over and scanned the signature block, he also affixed his name in all the appropriate places at a lightning pace and dutifully gave it to Davis.

Now, Capt. Olsen shifted his attention toward Natalie. The receipt was in the hands of a lawyer, and the young captain looked as if he were steeling himself for the coming storm of protest, but there was none. Likewise, she signed as quickly as the other two had, and the transfer of responsibility was completed instantly.

With the administrative battle won, the Norwegian paper warrior reassumed his inflated feeling of superiority like some Viking conqueror of old. In crisp military precision, he popped the clipboard under his arm and simultaneously presented the Jeep keys to Ms. Natalie Davis. As he watched the trio get into their new vehicle, Olsen couldn't help but think the entire episode was nothing more than a normal display of his wicked efficiency and extraordinary effectiveness. Even processing the paperwork and handing out the keys had been done in a ceremony so crisp to resemble a "Queen Ann Salute." Still, he should have checked the signatures. According to the receipt, Moe Howard, Curley Howard, and Larry Fine had just driven off with a brand new 1999 Jeep Cherokee.

The three hadn't been on the road for two miles before Tyler's mobile phone rang. "Longvue."

"Tyler Longvue," returned a thick Irish brogue.

"Who is this?"

"The man with your woman."

"If you harm her, by God I'll ... "

"Drop the theatrics," an unimpressed Branagh said. "You know what I want."

Longvue's phone battery had begun to fade. "You there? Hello? Look, my phone is going dead, talk fast; how do we do this?"

"That's what I like about you Yanks, business first. Hollywood Cafe in Udvar. Be there in one hour with the book and I'll give you the girl. Oh, and *boy-o*, make damn sure you come alone. Cheers."

"I need more than that, hello? Hello? Damn battery!"

Longvue dropped the phone back into his map case and looked at his watch. "Mark, get this thing to Beli Manastir as fast as you can."

"What are we going to do when we get there, Stickman?"

I'm working on it," said Tyler while he lit a smoke.

About six miles out of Osijek the three reached a checkpoint which led into the northern portion of the UN Transitional area. Usually the border crossing was a quiet place with a few military guards marshalling little traffic, but not today.

In the middle of the two-lane crossing point, a shouting contest was underway in three different languages between seven Croatian villagers and ten UN Pakistani border guards; something like the scene one would imagine at the Tower of Babel when God scattered the people, but with less order.

At the epicenter was a white armored personnel carrier separating two small cars. On the one side was a lime green ZAZ 965 and on the other, a rusty yellow Yugo pulling a trailer full of chickens. Obviously, there had been a wreck, and the confusion showed no sign of ending anytime soon.

Longvue leaned across the front seat as Burnwell slowed their vehicle to a stop. Davis immediately pulled out a map and looked for alternate routes. "Hell, everything off the main road is rigged to blow," she announced, "more damn mines around here than you can shake a stick at."

"We don't have time for this," replied Tyler, as he lit one cigarette off the other. "There's a big ol' hole in that screen door and it's too far to go back."

From the look on Burnwell's face, Davis saw he had had enough of the homespun wisdom.

"What is it with you two? Does everyone from Texas sound like Dan Rather?" With that he reached into his pocket and pulled out a wad of Kuna notes. "How about an idea instead of a cliché? Fork over what you've got."

At the exchange rate of 7.5 to 1, simply trading $100 for Kuna produced a pile of Croatian currency. Between the three of them, it seemed that they had a bucket full.

"Come on, Longvue, you speak the language," said the big man and the two of them hopped out of the Jeep and headed straight for the madness.

As Natalie watched the boys run off toward the crowd, she wrestled with indecision. Only a few minutes earlier the three of them had surmised there was a leak of information within the United Nations Mission because this Irish killer kept appearing and it wasn't by luck. They each agreed it was better not to contact anyone until they

Stephen Huey

had reached Beli Manastir and coordinated action with the US military contingent stationed in the town. But Davis started having second thoughts. She believed they were going to need more authority to get things done quickly, and she knew just who to call to get it, her boss.

While keeping an eye on her compatriots, Natalie called Charles Baxter and explained their situation in full detail.

"You were absolutely right to call me. I'll meet you in Beli Manastir in less than an hour. Have you contacted the military or the police yet?"

"No, sir, we think there's a leak."

"Good, don't call anyone else; we can't trust these bastards!"

In the distance, Natalie saw Tyler hand over the pile of money to an old man. It was evident they had reached some miraculous agreement because the mass of people, cars, and chickens suddenly parted, and there was a clean shot through the mayhem. Turning on their heels, the guys made double-time back to the Jeep.

"Okay, I need to get off the line. The fellas are headed back."

"Very good. You three get to Beli as quickly as you can and good luck!"

With Mark and Tyler back in the car, they sailed through the checkpoint while all the villagers smiled and waved. As the Jeep sped out of sight, the old Croat who made the deal with Longvue was counting the cash. He was joined by one of the other men.

"Zašto toliko novca,"
"Why so much money?"

118

"Da biste popravili moja kola zbog olupine,"
"To repair my car because of the wreck," the old one said.
"Kada ste se olupina?"
"When did you have a wreck?"
"Ne olupina, bio sam prodaje pilica."
"No wreck, I was selling chickens."

Vukovar: UNTAES Headquarters

Still mulling his options, Charles had been running different scenarios through their paces since he rang off. Regardless of the line of reason he followed, it always ended at the same fork in the road. *It's obvious the border guards have been paid off, so no one is going to be stopped at the crossings coming or going. And alerting the military now would only be a waste of time. In fact, if I call anyone now, I can't control the information. Everything I do has to be face-to-face.* Charles had reached the fork again; he made his decision and took it.

Opening his desk drawer, he removed his diplomatic passport and a .32 caliber Beretta Model 3032 Tom Cat. He then clapped on his overcoat and hat, shoved the pistol, phone, and passport into his jacket, and hustled out the door.

Over on the other side of the UN compound, Stephen Truman and Claire Anjou were also at the window observing the dissipating protestors. Claire saw Baxter walking to his gray S-Class Mercedes, and that's when a strange thought occurred to her.

"He looks so common, like an insurance salesman."

Stephen Huey

"I believe it is his job to go unnoticed."

"That's a good question, Stephen. What's Charles Baxter's job?"

"I'm not sure really, he does, things, I suppose," Truman said and kissed her on the cheek.

"What kind of things?"

"Bit of a mystery there as well. I've known him for almost thirty years and he's always done, well, things."

"Sounds like a spy."

"Oh I'm quite sure he is, Claire."

As they were about to turn away from the window and pursue more private matters, Anjou spotted a Jeep, which zipped down from the main gate, nearly hitting two people and Baxter's car before it skidded to a halt in front of the building. The door swung wide and out sprang an animated Margaret Lovejoy. Margaret watched Baxter drive away, then turned and dashed into the building.

"I believe our good doctor has gone mad," said Claire as she pulled the curtains together.

"It wouldn't be the first time," said Stephen. "I have a marvelous *Postup* I picked up in Zagreb; would you care for a glass?"

"Yes, I'd love one."

Turning on a small table lamp, Truman recovered the vintage 92 from inside his briefcase and walked over to the small two-seat bar. "Your comment about Margaret is not far from the mark. Since seeing her this morning, she's been acting strange."

Joining Stephen, Claire took a seat. "Well, it's a good thing the protest kept you two separated for most of the day."

Placing the stemware on the bar, Truman poured them each a glass and took a seat next to her. He raised his wineglass while never taking his eyes from hers. "Here's to us."

Three loud bangs disrupted any plans Stephen and Claire may have had in mind. Not only was it a shock to the romantic atmospherics, it was a shock to the well-established protocol. Everyone in the mission knew that when the chief's door was shut, he wasn't to be disturbed.

"Stephen, this can not wait a moment longer," followed the loud and authoritative voice of Col. Margaret E. Lovejoy. "I must speak with you this instant."

"Come in, Margaret, by all means."

"Would you like for me to leave?" inquired Anjou, seeing that the doctor was in no mood to be put off.

Before Truman could say a word, the headstrong colonel answered for him, "It makes no difference." Then, with neither hesitation nor apology, Lovejoy launched into her news.

chapter

ELEVEN

UN Transitional Area, North

Longvue's Jeep pulled into the parking lot of the Hollywood Bar. It was a dingy joint located near the Dubosevica-Udvar crossing which linked the UN protectorate to Hungary. The Hollywood was a relatively new Serbian dive, but like every other hold the Serbs had on the region, it was fading fast.

Alone, and carrying the map case containing the book, Longvue made his way to the door where he was stopped by a couple of Branagh's thugs. They checked him out, found him clean, and sent him in.

After stepping through the bead-shrouded door of the bar, Longvue's eyes landed on the photographs adorning the walls. There, mixed among black and white pictures of forgotten early-century bearded nobility, were full-color 5 x 7 action photos of the current Serbian icon, Nick Slaughter. To Tyler, it was a poignant display of the tragicomical essence of the once and future Yugoslavia.

A sensation on Serb TV, Slaughter was the main character in a sappy American detective series called *Tropical Heat*. Airing originally in the US for barely two seasons, Slaughter starred as a hard-drinking, cool guy, solving crime and pulling chicks. But the image and idea of the pony-tailed private eye morphed into something larger in the Balkans, particularly for the dissatisfied Serbian youth.

When students took to the streets of Belgrade in 1997 protesting Slobodan Milosevic, they sang *"Sloteru Niche, Serbia ti kliche,"* or "Nick Slaughter, Serbia Salutes You." Written by a punk rock band, it was the protestor's anthem in their fight against the cruelties and corruption of Milosevic. Somehow, this fictional detective became a true political force, and it pushed kids to brave police beatings and demand change. Unfortunately, Slobodan was still around, but so was Nick; maybe someone's days were numbered.

Longvue located the bar and made his way past several farmers who sat next to the fire. He ordered Rakija and found a table that faced the door. Shortly after he took his seat, Branagh appeared, holding a scared but resolute Nakamura, and they joined him.

Sitting opposite of Tyler, Nakamura was next to Branagh, who had his arm on the table with his coat across it.

"You're not much of a host," the Irish man started.

Longvue motioned to the bartender for another round, then looked at Kazuko. "Are you all right?"

Wide-eyed, she nodded in the affirmative.

"She couldn't be better," said Branagh. "Now let's get to the business of the day."

Longvue placed the map case on the table just as the drinks arrived. As he reached inside his coat pocket to pay, Tyler came to a dead stop. The barrel of a Walther PPK had popped up from underneath the Irish man's jacket, and it was pointed at his head. Slowly, he pulled cash out and handed it to the bartender.

"There we have it," said the red-headed assassin smugly and shook up a State Express 555 from its pack. He offered one to Longvue and the Irish killer lit them both. "Now, dear girl, take the books and show me the magic. And you, *boy-o*, keep your hands where I can see them."

Studying the cigarette brand, Tyler remarked, "If your partner had kept a better watch of the younger Mihjilo and not let him pull a pistol while he was at his desk, you wouldn't have had to shoot him so quickly. Still, I doubt if he would have ever told you where to find the book."

"How the devil did you know that?"

Clearly, Longvue's dead accurate account of the killing of Josip Mihjilo caught Branagh by total surprise. "There were no cameras; we checked. And you couldn't have seen anything. You arrived after ... " The assassin cut off his words as quickly as he had started. Eyeing the slim

Texan, a grin slowly stretched across his florid face. "For a moment I thought you'd done something clever. But it's nothing more than a guess."

"Oh, I never guess," said Longvue confidently. "And there's one more thing I'll give you for free. Your partner, the young tall one who likes to smoke Marlboros, I'd get rid of him. He's careless."

"Show's over," Branagh declared, in a voice annoyed with the detective. "No more of your carnival tricks, Tyler Longvue."

"No tricks; I'm just a policeman."

All at once a flap among the farmers erupted. One of the codgers, a hard looking old fellow with long gray and black hair, had taken the seat of another. It was difficult to tell if they were seriously arguing, or seriously drunk, or both. But the dust-up ended as quickly as it started when the grizzled long hair grudgingly relinquished his position. He stood with a stoop and was obviously crippled, another unfortunate recipient of war's collateral damage. His tattered long black wool coat couldn't hide the fact his right arm hung uselessly. But the malady most pronounced was a deep scar, which ran the length of his face from forehead to jaw. Every old man around the fire knew that could have been his fate. So, another chair appeared and peace returned. At Longvue's table, though, the entire episode had passed without their notice because all attention was on Nakamura.

Despite the noise or the gun pressed into her side, Kazuko's excitement couldn't be checked and took over as she unraveled the code. First, she wrote down a long series of numbers taken from Old Mihjilo's book. Next, she changed the numerals into letters using some formula she had derived from Young Mihjilo's book.

"It's a substitution code with an intricate twist. You see the value of the words, they double, making the algorithm for this cipher a series of three."

"Damn it, girl, I don't care. Just tell me how to read the thing. I can make no sense of it," Branagh snapped unimpressed with cryptography.

"That's because there's a final part, but it's not in the books."

"Where is it?"

"In my head."

"Bitch, don't play games or you'll watch your boyfriend be splattered on the wall."

"But not too soon, yes?"

Surprised, Branagh turned toward the deep Russian voice for less than a second, but it was all the time Longvue needed. He snatched the killer's weapon and twisted it free while simultaneously, a Soviet-era PSS 6P28 Silent pistol jammed itself deep into the Irishman's neck.

At the other end of the pistol was a ragged but smiling Zavisha. As it turned out, the stooped and disfigured soul, who had earlier caused such a commotion, was the big Russian playing a part.

Tyler was impressed with his Russian pal. Not only was his timing spot on, but his disguise was a masterpiece. Every good cop knew the best way to hide was to make people not want to look. Therefore, Zavisha's long greasy hair, pronounced handicap, and hideous full-face scar were as effective in concealment as some sci-fi cloaking device.

"You'll never leave here alive," said the captured assassin looking in vain for a way out.

"Ah, you refer to your friends, outside," answered Nikita as he stretched back into his full frame. "I will deal with them presently."

Suddenly, an enigmatical voice croaked its way into the conversation. "Good work, gentlemen."

Like four characters in a melodrama, all at the table turned in silence to observe the dumpy frame of Charles Baxter unbuttoning his topcoat. Even Zavisha's spectacular deception paled in comparison to the sight of the rumpled State Department Officer, who moved into the seat next to Longvue and took charge.

"What do we have here? Ms. Nakamura, you okay?"

"I'm fine, Sir."

"Very good; and these must be Mihjilo's books, I take it."

Baxter picked them up, flipped through them, and put them into his overcoat pocket.

"Yes, sir."

"Charles, you will permit," started Zavisha, "how did you find us?"

"We can talk about this back at HQ, but right now we need to get out of here. The bombing has started, and we're too damn close to the Serbian border. I'd rather avoid being hit by one of NATO's not-so-smart bombs. Even the noblest man's meat is inferior to pork."

Branagh immediately flashed at the disheveled bureaucrat. Seeing the eyes, Charles returned the favor and the two moved from a look, to a stare, to a glare, to daggers.

"I've heard that before."

"I'm sure you have," countered Baxter, "Mark Twain said it."

"No, it was you on the phone."

"I assure you it was Twain, and he couldn't have been on the phone. Who is this idiot anyway? Go ahead and take him."

With that, two sets of large muscular arms reached around Branagh and plucked him from his seat. Cuffed, gagged, and hooded, the Irish fellow was dispatched in the blink of an eye. It was an efficient display of the exceptional work of GROM, Polish Special Forces. Baxter had brought along a squad, and these cats didn't take no for an answer.

GROM had been sent to the mission to catch war criminals, and they were good at their jobs; this was simply recreational activity for these boys.

Outside the bar was no different. The scene was quiet and under control. In a matter of minutes, the six elite soldiers in black fatigues had disposed of the hooligans standing guard and secured the area. Nikita and Tyler exited the bar and just behind them were Charles and Kazuko, wrapped deep in conversation.

"Ms. Nakamura, I'd like you to ride with me. I want to discuss the books more." As they arrived at his car, Baxter opened the door for her and called out to Longvue, "We'll meet you in Beli Manastir." Longvue waved in acknowledgement while he and the largest member of GROM placed the cuffed Branagh in the back seat of his Cherokee.

Before getting into the Jeep, Longvue yelled across the parking lot, "Kazuko, did you notice the cigarettes? State Express 555s; that's how I knew it was our guy from Zagreb."

"You amaze me," she shouted back while getting into the car with Baxter.

Tyler muttered to himself, "Elementary, my dear."

"Comrade, do you need that I follow while you deposit our Irish friend?" asked Zavisha.

"No. That mountain of a Polish guy sitting next to him is praying that knucklehead will do something stupid. I think he'll behave. And good work, old man. We couldn't have done this without you."

"Yes, well, you're welcome," offered the Russian lawyer in a disappointed tone. "I'll return now to Vukovar, *ciao*."

Longvue was vexed by these words. *This was a triumph*, he thought, as his friend walked away, *yet he sounded whipped*. But decoding the inner workings of a post Soviet brain wasn't the task at hand. So, Tyler got into the Jeep with his prisoner and drove off to the jail in Beli Manastir.

Nothing had happened in the village of Petolvac, as usual. It was a small pleasant hamlet and miles away from all the action that had just taken place at the Hollywood Bar in Udvar. But it was the location where Mark Burnwell and Natalie Davis had been instructed by Charles Baxter to wait. They were told to stay put, in radio silence, until contacted for movement. This meant no phone calls and no radio transmissions. Baxter said security was a problem, and he didn't want to chance a stray conversation fouling up the plan to rescue Nakamura.

Burnwell and Davis thought it smart and did as instructed, for an hour. But after sixty minutes and no communication with the outside world, the charming surroundings wore thin, along with their patience. Matters didn't improve any when they decided to break the silence, but were unable to raise anyone on the phone or the radio. The couple took off for Udvar.

Just as Burnwell made it to the main road, a short distance ahead a gray Mercedes had topped the hill at breakneck speed headed their way. Zipping past, Davis said, "That's Baxter. Where the hell is he going?"

A couple of minutes later, Longvue's Cherokee appeared. Burnwell stopped and got out to flag down the Stickman. Davis remained in the vehicle and her mobile finally rang.

"Davis ... yes, Mr. Truman, we just saw Baxter, he rolled by us a few seconds ago, headed toward Beli Manastir ... No, I couldn't tell who was with him ... Yes sir, I tried Longvue's phone, but I couldn't get a hold of him. In fact, I couldn't call anyone. There was no reception," Natalie said and paused for a moment. *That's why he wanted us to wait in Petolvac*, she reasoned to herself, *it's a communications black hole.*

Even though Baxter was driving at speeds in excess of 110 mph, he was on his mobile phone. "Yes, he's on his way to Beli Manastir. Is all prepared for our visitor?" When the answer came, satisfaction creased the lips of the Old Balkan hand in the form of a smile, something rare for Baxter. "Very good, *ciao*."

Meanwhile, deep within her alternate universe, Nakamura's toil was giving way to the wonder of her discovery. At that moment, nothing else mattered to her except the task at hand. Even more intoxicating was the opportunity to explain it, so she began.

"I kept trying to associate the verse, 'in death the one is now three as they return to their mother.' Then it came to me; it all made sense!"

"Okay," replied Baxter with little enthusiasm.

"You see, Mihjilo chose Cerberus, a three headed hellhound, as his stamp. When he died, the memory of him became Cerberus, the one is now three. And Night is the mother of Death, 'who lives to the West beyond the glorious ocean.' The knot was untied; it was such a clever riddle!"

"If you say so, Ms. Nakamura."

Though beaming with her breakthrough she saw Baxter was lost, so she took a breath to calm and started again.

"Okay. Using the codebooks, we arrive at these large numbers. Obviously they need to be made smaller to fit into the key. This is where I use the verse. According to the first part, in death the one is now three, I divide the number by three. Then, with the second part, as they return to their mother, I divide by 270. This formula gives a set of numbers corresponding to the key. From there it's a simple substitution."

"Dividing by three because of the wolf thing, I guess I understand, but how the blazes did you come up with 270?"

Here she took on extra delight because this part was most difficult for her to crack. "In Greek Mythology, Night is the mother of Death, who lives West beyond the glorious ocean. West on a compass is … "

"Two hundred and seventy degrees. Excellent work, Ms. Nakamura, but where does it all lead?"

With attention returned to the books, her analysis continued. "Most of it deals with banking transfers, ten separate Swiss accounts, and shipping information, none of it current. But there are two peculiarities. The entries stopped in the early 80s."

"Which corresponds with Tito's death," Baxter said. "And the other?"

Nakamura frowned and wrote out a long string of numbers. "I don't know, it's a series of eight digits followed by some kind of, story?" She worked the code a bit longer.

"Yeah, a story about gold and silver coins. And these, these numbers appear to be directions?"

After deciphering more, a most unlikely location revealed itself to the Japanese code breaker. "These are directions to Antuovac."

"Antunovac," exclaimed Baxter. "That village is so heavily mined, no one can get in there; it's impossible, it's a deathtrap, it's, it's brilliant! Ms. Nakamura, that's a treasure map."

"Then the stories are true?"

"I believe they are. Please, please continue."

By this time it was early afternoon, and Baxter had crossed the checkpoint and was back in Croatia proper. He'd turned off the main road and was zipping the back way through tiny obscure places where few folks traveled. Still, somewhere between the villages of lost and forgotten, a black unmarked UN Police Land Cruiser had clocked the flying diplomat way over the limit and attempted to pull him over. Still unconscious to the events of the outside world, Kazuko kept her focus on her work.

"We've picked up a companion," Baxter said of the black cruiser.

"Who is it?"

"Don't know and, considering the way things are, I don't want to find out."

When Charles' vehicle hit the Dunav Bridge in Osijek, it was piled up with the usual thick line of traffic. Rather than slowing down, he increased his speed and weaved wildly through the congestion. Amazingly, the chase car was able to do the same. Even several more quick turns onto crowded city streets proved no advantage for the fleeing gray Mercedes. These UN cops wouldn't quit. Then Osijek's open-air market came into view. It was thriving, packed, and just what Baxter needed, a crowd to get lost in, so he plunged ahead.

With Kiosks lining both sides of the street, the bazaar had been in continual operation for the last fifty years. Appropriately, this gray marketplace thrived under the shadows of Soviet era high-rise apartment buildings while government officials gave a wink-and-a-nod to its illegal commerce. Like so many dichotomies in eastern Europe, this free-market was both an anathema to the

Communist system and one of the few institutional success stories in the region.

Turning down the main drag, the gray Mercedes plowed its way into and through a mass of humanity. Carts of goods were knocked over. Citizens had to leap out of the way. Screams and curses confronted and followed Baxter's car as it mowed through the gauntlet.

Vegetables, fruit, rocks, cans, anything people could get their hands on was hurled at the reckless auto. The back window cracked from the deluge, but Baxter kept going and made it out the other end. By this time, the normally jovial mood of merchants and patrons had switched to the unbridled anger of a mob seeking revenge. Even those living in the overlooking apartments had come out onto their balconies and joined the furor. All this was waiting on the black Land Cruiser as it turned the corner and waded in.

Before the black Toyota got a quarter of the way down the avenue, the people had unloaded their fury. Vegetables, mud, fruit, trash, sticks, bottles, rocks, even a few gunshots rained down on the Toyota. The ceaseless torrent blinded the driver, who crashed the Cruiser into a lamp pole. When the car came to a stop, two uniformed UN police monitors, a Kenyan and an American, bailed out and ran for their lives. Close on their heels was the frenzied mob in full chase.

Stopped just up the street, cleaning debris from the windscreen, Baxter saw the mayhem unfolding a few blocks away. In a voice that sounded unconcerned, he remarked, "Looks like a scene from a bad Frankenstein movie."

Seeing the cops in trouble, Kazuko turned on the two-way radio and keyed the microphone, "Vukovar base, Vukovar base, over."

Baxter hopped back in, snatched the radio from her hand, and snapped off the cord. No words were spoken, there was no need, the empty cold of Baxter's small dark eyes told Kazuko everything. It was he. Charles Baxter, the undersized round rumpled man, was behind it all. He had sent the assassins, he had ordered the murders, and now he had the books. Tires squealed and the Mercedes was off.

chapter

TWELVE

Antunovac, UN Transitional Area

Abandoned and left for dead, this once thriving Croatian village was now quiet, empty, and destroyed. Along the tree-lined narrow street leading to the village center, there had once stood a tidy line of near storybook homes. Now, there was only a pile of knocked-down, burned-out ruins, which flanked the way. Of what remained standing, large caliber bullet holes crisscrossed the exteriors and served as a reminder of the horror. The aftermath of this destruction was emptiness, and it was eerie. There was no sound of life, only the hollow rustle of wind as it traveled through tall weeds.

Charles Baxter's car stopped at the stone barriers and double strung array of land mine warning signs that barred entrance into the lifeless hamlet. Doors on both sides of the Mercedes opened, and Baxter and Nakamura got out. She held papers in her hands to guide her through the minefield; he held a gun in his to make sure she did it. Before she set off, he handed her a few sticks of colored chalk.

"I knew my artistic skills would pay off; you'll need this for your journey."

He gave her the chalk and waved her forward to the edge of the town. "Now, it's time to test your findings. Take the map, mark your steps, and proceed."

Baxter took a seat on the hood of his car and watched as Nakamura checked and double-checked before taking her first step. She picked up a foot, reviewed her notes, and returned her foot to its starting position.

"We haven't all day," said the annoyed State officer. Still, Kazuko could only stand and stare at what was in front of her.

The sharp report of a small caliber round skipped off the pavement to her right. "Get on with it!"

Nakamura had no choice. She stepped off, and survived. After a few more tentative steps, and marking her way, she realized she had indeed broken the code.

A half hour passed and she was only seventy-five yards into the village, but according to her calculations, she had arrived at her destination. Kazuko faced a large home that, for the most part, had been spared the fate of its neighboring structures. It was shot up, to be sure, but most of it was still intact. A stone fence surrounded the property, and a short concrete walkway led to the double door threshold of the old place. Amazingly, there was a large two-section floor-to-ceiling bay window that spanned the left side of the house. It was impossible to see through because of the accumulated dirt and dust, but it was the only pane of unbroken glass in the entire town.

"This is it," she cried.

"Good job, Ms. Nakamura, keep going. You're doing fine."

"From here it's rather complicated."

"You're a smart girl, mark it off. Let's go." Baxter got up from his seat and followed the chalk outline that snaked its way through the street.

At the gateway she studied the short path. There were no obstacles and, according to her notes, it was a clean walk to the doorway. This was suspicious, she thought. *Why was this so easy?* Arriving at the portico, she discovered the answer.

Confronted with two doors, she had to choose. One or both could be rigged to explode.

"Why are we stopping?"

"We? It's me up here and I don't know which door to open. The books didn't say."

"Don't get so testy; it fogs the thinking. And you have plenty of it to do right about now. It's the classic lady or the tiger. Good luck." Baxter stepped back a few paces but motioned with his pistol for her to continue.

Now, her life had come down to a 50/50 chance. *It wasn't fair*, she thought, but that soon changed. Her brain went into hyper-drive, trying to think of something, anything.

"Come on, dear, I don't want to shoot you, but if I must, I will," said Charles, who was retreating to be clear of the possible blast. "We don't have all day."

Not looking back, Kazuko reached down and took hold of the left handle. As she applied muscle pressure to twist it open, she froze.

Epiphany.

Gently, she released the left and, without hesitation, twisted the right handle down; a mechanical click, the door latch dropped, nothing. Slowly she pushed the Serbian hardwood slightly ajar; again nothing. Peering inside, she gauged her luck. On the left side was a booby trap set with C4 explosives. Saying nothing to Baxter, Nakamura entered the home.

Beli Manastir, UN Transitional Area North: UN Police Station

With his feet up on the desk, Burnwell flipped through the latest propaganda spouted in the weekly UNTAES bulletin. It was a highly controlled and highly selective seven-day rag that was good for a laugh, provided one's humor was dark. Longvue, on the other hand, continued to pace as he'd been doing since their arrival forty-five minutes ago. After depositing Branagh in jail, the two had been waiting on Charles and Kazuko at the Beli Manastir station.

"Where the hell can they be?" said Tyler, checking his watch to the time displayed on the two-way radio dispatch base. He'd tried several times to reach Charles via the airwaves, phone and radio, no luck; In fact, it had been so quiet around the station, the officer monitoring the radio left without asking either Tyler or Mark to stand in for him.

"Give Natalie another call."

"No, it's only been ten minutes; besides, she'll call if she finds them," replied Burnwell, not lowering the newspaper from his face.

"We need to do something."

"Like what, Stickman?"

"I'll be damned."

"You're well on your way," Mark said, as he folded the local rag and searched for another. Frustrated, Tyler sat in the dispatcher's chair and lit a smoke. On the desk in front of him was a hand-written log of all radio traffic. In an attempt to get his mind off the present situation, Longvue half-heartedly read over the record. Less than a quarter of the way down the page his eyes fixed on an unexpected entry.

"Damn it!"

"We gotta work on your vocabulary."

"No, fathead," Longvue shouted as he jumped from his chair. "A police patrol spotted Baxter's car outside of Antunovac almost thirty minutes ago. It's recorded in the log." Equally energized, Burnwell tossed the paper and flew out the door with his partner.

A good bit of time had passed since Kazuko disappeared into the house, and Baxter had grown anxious with the dead air. Out of boredom, he inched back carefully along the chalk line to the front of the house. "Ms. Naka-mura, I'm tired of waiting!" But his bark was met with con-tinued silence. More time dragged by and this was some-thing Charles knew he was running low on. He had to act. So, with eyes and feet zeroed in on the colored streaks of chalk along the concrete path to the door, he headed in.

Once inside the house, Baxter paused in the vesti-bule for the strange sight. Years of dust accumulation, which swirled in a cloud around his feet, had turned the interior into a thick blanket of gray. The grimy powder was a smooth, undisturbed cover on everything except for the new footprints, which shuffled off to the right from where he stood. It was evident the owners left in a hurry, from what he saw. The residence appeared fully furnished. Immediately to his left were the explosives and a short hallway leading into a living room with an old large walnut Spanish Chest in the center. Beyond the chest was another hallway filled with hazy outside light that seeped through the near opaque window.

"Nakamura!" There was no answer. To his right, the chalk path was visible through the grit and filth, so he fol-lowed it.

Hid away behind an oversized chair in the living room, Kazuko held her place until Baxter made the corner and out of the line of sight. Then, quickly and quietly, she climbed atop the ancient chest, faced the muted daylight filled hallway that led into the living room, and waited for her hunter. As each step brought the killer closer, her breathing became more labored. Then the chubby little executioner appeared. Bathed in the gloomy light of the corridor he was rumpled, enraged, and armed.

Seeing his prey perched expressionlessly, Baxter raised his weapon and started her way. But when he looked down, his motion was stopped.

At the entry to the living room, there were three different dusty paths, sketched out in chalk, from the hallway to the Spanish Chest. Additionally, each of the trails had a large gap in it before reaching her.

"This is foolish, young lady," he yelled.

Nervous but resolute, she replied strongly, "maybe, but this place is full of traps. Those breaks can be a clear path or a land mine pressure plate. If you want this treasure, you have to choose, lady or the tiger, remember?"

"Look, we don't have much time; we'll share the wealth."

"You want me to trust you?"

"Do you have a choice?"

Pulling both codebooks from her coat, "yes, I have these."

Outside, a UN Jeep rolled quietly to a stop. Burnwell had killed the engine and coasted the final twenty-five yards to the village. He and Longvue exited, armed with a M-16 and Glock 17 respectively. They moved cautiously to a vantage point that offered cover. From there they saw Baxter's Mercedes was empty, so they moved swiftly and silently to the car. After checking it, they stepped to the edge of the village and followed the chalk line path with their eyes. They both were well aware it was a stroll through a minefield.

"Let's wait for backup," Mark whispered. "We can set up a sniper position near the Jeep."

Stephen Huey

"Good plan. He's gotta come out."

With two loud cracks from a Beretta .32 caliber pistol coming from inside a house, the plan changed. No words were necessary; the boys knew what they had to do.

Other than two fresh bullet holes in the wall above Nakamura's head, not much had changed inside the house.

"Damn it, tell me the way!

"So you can, so you can kill me?"

"You bitch!"

"Kazuko, get down! Drop it Baxter!"

From the door, Longvue was unable to get off a shot because Kazuko was in the line of fire. Instinctively, Charles jumped back against the wall in the hallway for cover and was able to keep a bead on Nakamura.

"Don't move, Longvue, or by God I'll kill this little bitch!"

"Stay down, Kazuko, stay down! Baxter, you don't have a chance. Drop the weapon and show me your hands!"

It was here, in a true pressure cooker situation, Charles Augustus Baxter III demonstrated what had long made him so successful in his field; he simply relaxed. Maybe one person in 10,000 was able to do this. It was utterly bizarre, but so was Charles.

"Good job, we have a standoff. Now what, genius? You've backed yourself into a corner."

He was right, and Longvue knew it. Looking around, the lean policeman tried to come up with a plan, but options were remarkably thin upon the ground. Nakamura was hugging the top of the chest, Burnwell had taken a knee on the street, and the ghostly quiet of the village had returned, jacking up the tension on all. Well, on all except one; to Longvue, it sounded as if Baxter was enjoying this.

"Mr. Policeman, you have two choices: Either I walk out with her alive or she and I get carried out dead. I'll give you some time to make up your mind. You've got ten seconds, nine ... "

The dumpy diplomat had him. All Tyler saw was a round shadow painted on a dusty floor. He had no shot, he had no time, he had no, then it came to him. "Charles," shouted Longvue, "what's a six letter word for an opening in a wall?"

"You're an idiot," returned Baxter and resumed. "Five, four, three." Then he turned his head and said, "Window."

Luck ran out for the big bay when it shattered and was followed by the powerful crack of an M16. The 5.56 round breaking the glass pierced the neck, struck the thoracic vertebrae, and ended the luck of one Charles Baxter as well. Muscles gave way, and the diplomat was dead before he hit the floor. Outside, Burnwell lowered his smoking rifle and the strange silence returned.

After seeing the carcass drop, Longvue stepped off directly toward it.

"Don't move," screamed Kazuko. Freezing mid-step, the over-anxious Texan gently set his foot back in place.

"There are enough explosives in the hallway to level the block," she said. "Follow the path closely the other way and come help me with this thing."

Arriving at the pile that was Baxter, Longvue picked up his weapon and noticed the three paths to his friend. "How do I get in there?"

She hopped down from atop the chest. "Come on, this room is safe; I drew the lines to slow him down."

"So, is this what I think it is?"

"You tell me, Stickman."

Nakamura threw back the lid, and there laid the wealth of centuries. Inside the chest were hundreds and hundreds of gold and silver coins from the Ottoman Empire; precious stones as large as the Archduke Joseph Diamond; ruby and sapphire-studded Eastern Orthodox religious symbols; cups, rings, pearls, all from the Royal House of Karadjordjevic, and all priceless.

"Jesus, Mary, and Joseph."

She smiled at his choice of words. "Yeah, it's a miracle."

Burnwell entered the front door, immediately saw the treasure, and his entire body snapped into a highly animated contortion.

"Wa-who!"

And just as Longvue, he raised his foot and was about to step off in their direction.

"STOP!"

By the time the UN crowd arrived in Antunovac, all the chalk markings had been removed from the street. The single road into the village was now packed with vehicles and personnel. Yellow crime scene tape was up along with two unfriendly looking Belgian soldiers to keep the gawkers manageable, especially the police. It's hardwired into their DNA; when a dead body hits the ground, it's like a disturbance in the force. Cops feel it and they flock to it just to get a peek.

Longvue made his way over to Truman upon his arrival at the scene.

"Baxter's body is still inside the house."

"All right, Tyler. I'll get this area swept clear of mines and have it recovered. Oh, I don't know if you've heard; the man you dropped off at Beli Manastir prison appears to have killed himself."

"Jesus, Baxter certainly knew how to cover his tracks."

"Well, that's certainly gone to the grave. As well as this unpleasant business; excuse me while I get these people started."

Casually unzipping his coat, Tyler took out a smoke and lit it.

"I wouldn't do that just yet, Mr. Truman; we've got some cleaning up to do in there."

Stephen gave a perplexed look. Longvue moved closer and opened his jacket a bit wider, exposing a solid gold crucifix studded with flawless rubies at the ends.

"The stories about the book and the treasure are true," the Texan continued in a low voice. "There's more inside; much more."

Longvue zipped up, and the two men looked around at all the people on the scene. "This could get way out of control, Mr. Truman."

"Right you are. Major!" The Belgian commander ran over to the UN Chief. "Post your men in front of the village. No one is to enter without my permission."

chapter

THIRTEEN

UNTAES Headquarters, Vukovar

It was Friday, winter, and late afternoon, so most every UN office in the compound was closed, dark, and deserted. Zavisha's heavy footsteps in the gloomy corridors would have been the only sound but for the racket pouring from the last room in the east wing. Following the hullabaloo through the hallways was simple for the big Russian. The surprise came when he arrived at the open doorway and found that only four people were generating such a cacophony.

With the second bottle of Chopin Vodka sitting outside on the window ledge cooling, Kazuko, Tyler, Mark, and Margaret had been crammed into Nakamura's broom closet of an office for more than an hour-and-a-half cackling about the prior day's events.

"I apologize for my lateness, but I come with gifts," said Nikita. From inside his briefcase he produced yet another bottle of Chopin and a fine container of Beluga Caviar. He had also stopped by the chow hall and picked up some pedestrian crackers, but at $500 a tin, this Caspian Sea delicacy would make wood chips taste extraordinary.

"Glad you could make it, old boy. Let me help you with that," replied Longvue, as he retrieved a vodka bottle from outside and put the new one on the ledge to chill. He poured a shot for his companion, put the liquor back outdoors, and all raised their glasses in salute.

"Drag in another chair from the office next door and stay awhile," Longvue called out.

"Unfortunately, I can not," replied Nikita. "My affairs take me to Paris on this short notice. Claire and I are to meet with UN lawyers about the books, no less."

"Seems everyone's leaving," chimed in Margaret. "Stephen's off to New York and Kazuko's on her way to Zagreb."

"I'll be here, Maggie," interjected Burnwell with a dreamy sort of half-smile.

"That's nice, dear."

"Why to Zagreb?" inquired the Russian as he popped a cigarette into his mouth.

"It'll be safer for her."

"Which I still think is over-reaction, Tyler. Baxter's dead, and the books as well as the treasure are in the custody of UNTAES."

"But you still hold the keys to unlocking them," said Margaret. "Best to separate the two of you for now."

"Most assuredly right," confirmed Zavisha, "but there hasn't been constructed the single point of failure, correct? Another has the key, perhaps?"

"No, there's not, 'the single point of failure,'" Nakamura said while affecting a crummy Russian accent. "In addition to me, there are two others who know the key to unlocking the code books."

"I think you're saying more than you should, Kazuko."

"And I think this situation is being handled all wrong, Tyler."

"And I think you're both right," Margaret said as she reached between them and took some caviar. As always, the colonel had a way of taking charge of things without offending. "The books are locked safe and so is the key. Let's keep it that way for a few days longer."

"If I must," said the miffed human rights officer, "but it doesn't follow."

"I agree, but there's a lot that doesn't follow," Mark proffered. "For instance, Nikita, this has been bugging the hell out of me. How did you follow these two from Zagreb to Osijek to Udvar? No one else could find these guys."

"KGB method."

"Meaning, I called him daily," deadpanned Tyler.

"Now, you know all and I must be excused," said Zavisha and finished his drink.

Stephen Huey

Kazuko threw open the window and pulled in a freezing bottle of Chopin as Margaret lined up the shot glasses for another round. All bid their Russian friend farewell and Longvue saw him to the hallway.

"Meeting with the beautiful Claire Anjou, and in Paris no less. Is this business or pleasure?"

"A beautiful woman, no doubt. But Tyler, she's lawyer, I'm lawyer, we are meeting more lawyers. My friend, where is the pleasure?"

After watching his comrade until he vanished in the dark passageway, Tyler turned to go back into the office, but paused as the door swung open to the hall. He looked at it for a moment, then turned his gaze to Nakamura's somewhat intoxicated eyes.

"Kazuko, something just occurred to me. When you got to the double doors at the house, the book didn't tell you which door to pick, right?"

"You're correct, Stickman."

"So, how did you figure it out?"

Longvue instantly recognized that this was what she had been waiting for, another chance to explain. She took a moment, then started her discourse.

"Well, it all became clear when I remembered that 'night is the mother of death, who lives west beyond the glorious ocean.' On a map, west is to the left. So, if death travels in that direction, life must be the opposite way. Therefore, I opened the door on the right."

"That's amazing," said Burnwell, gobbling up the last bit of caviar. "You make it all sound so simple."

"It doesn't always work out so well," she said. "Things get missed."

"Yeah, like Baxter," shot back Mark. "Somehow that rat bastard got missed for years. And I'm not real sure how we caught him."

"Well, most of it was your doing, dear," said Margaret, "albeit roundabout."

"Albeit. I love it when you talk British."

"It's called English, but pay attention; you're the leading character in this story. The saga of Charles Baxter started the night all those poor devils came pouring into the hospital. Turns out the old man who tried to shoot Mihjilo also knew our Mr. Baxter. He said Charles was a double-agent, a colonel in the KGB, and had been working for the Russians since the early 1970s."

"And you believed this guy?"

"On its face I should say not, Mr. Longvue. One hears too many fairy stories here in the Balkans. But these were his dying words and, as we all know, they carry weight. So, I conducted an experiment."

Clearing a spot on the desk, Col. Dr. Margaret Lovejoy moved the shot glasses around like she was explaining a tabletop military exercise.

"My plan was to tell Charles about the Irishman and the book and gauge his reaction. I did so, but the results were disappointing. The information seemed to register nothing with him, one way or the other. I thought my test a failure before it had started. But then our hero staggered in from Udvar and everything came to light."

"I'll be honest, Doc, I have no idea what I said to you that night."

"So, we're not getting married?"

Uncharacteristically, Lovejoy had caught the flat-foot, flat footed. And with a grin, she continued.

"At first, Mark's inebriated story about this Irish and American assassin team passing through the border in the dead of night, I was ready to put down as just another porky. But when he said the Yank was a Russian Colonel, I had it; my proof. Mr. Burnwell, you cracked it."

But there was no satisfaction to be found on Mark's face. In fact, his countenance was something between confused and painful. "I don't understand. He had the books, Swiss Bank accounts worth millions."

"A billion," chimed in Kazuko, which earned a stern look from Tyler.

"Wow! Now, it's even more confusing," said Burnwell, shaking his head in utter disbelief. "The guy had a billion dollars in his hands, but it wasn't enough. Baxter had to have the treasure as well. He had to have it all."

"A fat bastard, that one," Dr. Lovejoy said. "We were in luck. Now, all the treasure and all its complications belong to the people. Maybe it's not so lucky."

"Well, that's half right. The locals have the treasure, but the books with the bank accounts have turned into a lottery on steroids. Anyone who can spell Yugoslavia is laying a claim."

"And as I said, it's being handled all wrong, Tyler. The treasure and the books belong here, to the people."

"You're right, Kazuko, of course," said Margaret with pessimism in her voice. "By the way, where are the books?"

"Locked safely in the Bank of Vukovar," Mark said as he filled the glasses again.

"Hardly an address that inspires confidence," quipped the doctor.

Osijek, Croatia

Two flashes of yellow light silently pierced the darkness of the single penthouse suite atop the Hotel Osijek. In the next instant, the apartment's floor-to-ceiling glass shattered, followed by another flash of yellow and the sound of a pistol. It was exactly 1:30 am, and from a height of exactly 130 feet, the dead body of Claire Anjou started its descent toward the snow-covered earth. Her twelve story journey ended less than four seconds later when it slammed to a halt near the river embankment. No one saw it, and no one heard it, but it happened. Just like the tragedy pictured in Brueghel's *Icarus*, the world ignored the suffering and continued.

chapter

FOURTEEN

Osijek, Croatia

For the normally dreary and gray time of the season, the morning was an aberration of spectacular note. It was cold, to be sure, but the blow of searing icy wind had taken the day off, and not a single cloud was parked in the crisp blue sky. Such was the perfect winter's day for the crowd milling about on the snowy stretch between the Hotel Osijek and the River Drava. But it wasn't a festival that brought them to the water's edge, nor was it the lifeless remains of Claire Anjou; it was the lure of money.

As he pushed his way through the herd, Longvue showed his ID to a chunky Croatian Police Sergeant and ducked under the yellow tape that barely controlled the pedestrian parade. He joined Burnwell, who was standing next to the spot where Anjou had been found.

"You know what's weird?" started the Mormon. "That chick fell 130 feet. She's got a bullet hole punched in her chest, there was a mark across the left side of her face where she had been struck, and still."

"I know," said Longvue. "And she still looked good. Any witnesses?"

"None. But we did find one of those books."

"You're kidding," replied Tyler as he shook loose a Marlboro from the pack. "Where was it?"

"It was about a yard below her feet. Right there where that stake is with the yellow tape. It was next to the pistol she used on Stephen."

Tyler lit his smoke and studied the area around the body. "It doesn't make any sense, I thought they loved each other."

"Yeah, that's what everybody thought," said Burnwell. "I guess greed had her by the throat, but in the end they both lost."

"You said you found one book. Is the other missing?"

"Yeah. Best we can make of it, she had them both when she went out the window. We've searched the area, twice, and came up empty, so it must have gone in the drink. That's why all those folks are out there."

Mark pointed at the ever-growing flotilla of Croatian police boats and privately owned crafts that bobbed across the top of the murky Drava.

"As soon as the word got out, every canoe on the river paddled out here to drag the bottom, looking to find that missing book. This story has wings."

"Wings? Hell, more like a jet engine. After I saw Kazuko off at the UN Compound in Zagreb this morning, the cab driver who took me to the train station, even he was talking about this incident. Who found her anyway?"

"We got lucky there," Burnwell continued. "One of the hotel maids stumbled onto the body coming in early this morning. She knew Claire was UN. When she got to the hotel, she saw a couple of the Irish guys, Declan and Mike, and told them."

"Those are two good cops. How the hell did this happen?" asked Tyler as he turned his gaze to the crowd that continued to grow.

"Oh, the boys did everything right; secured the scene, bagged and tagged the evidence, started a canvass, but then they notified HQ."

"And that's when the wheels fell off?"

"Right you are, Tyler. Word got out about the book and it turned into this."

"Jesus, what a circus."

"Oh, you ain't seen nothing, Stickman. Wait till we go up to the penthouse. They should have charged admission. A ton of folks have trampled through it."

"Who the hell is in charge of the investigation?"

"Investigation? You high? Everyone out here knows if they find that book, they're rich. Nobody cares about the body found here or the other two upstairs."

Two young UN policemen plowed their way through the gaggle and arrived at the crime scene.

"All done, are we?" piped up one of the British Bobbies.

Tyler turned to the portly police sergeant who was deep in a conversation with two of his junior officers.

"Jeste li završili?"

"Are you finished?"

Without stopping his dialog, the beefy cop glanced at the inquiring Texan and signaled with his hand in a rapid shooing motion to leave.

"All right, fellas, let's wrap it up," said Longvue, as he stepped back and looked up at the high-rise hotel. "Mark, you said the book and the gun were found together below her feet?"

"That's right, why?"

"I don't know, seems odd," replied Longvue while he looked from the stake marking the location up to the top floor of the hotel, then back again trying to decipher the invisible. "Come on, let's go upstairs."

When Longvue and Burnwell stepped off the elevator to Stephen Truman's penthouse apartment, they were met by two large Croatian police officers. Both were seated at the desk that had once been the post of Truman's bodyguard, and both were unhappy. Being stuck on guard duty wasn't where they wanted to be when the Yugoslavian wheel of fortune was spinning just outside. The two merely glanced at the UN identification cards presented by Tyler and Mark, and mechanically they were waved through. Security for the crime scene wasn't the best, but it was better than it had been earlier in the day.

Normally, in these circumstances, the Croatian authorities allowed the United Nations to take care of matters in-house. It was an arrangement that usually worked well. But when the local cops learned that one of the treasure books was up for grabs, convention was tossed aside and the Croats took control. There was one problem, though; the lag time between their inaction and action had been costly to the crime scene.

After Tyler opened the door to the penthouse, he saw that Mark hadn't exaggerated in the least. From top to bottom, the apartment had been ransacked.

"Nice. I don't understand why they're guarding this place. Do we have any idea how many people have been in here since the incident?"

"No idea," returned Burnwell as he made his way toward the shattered window. "For hours, people skipped their way in and out of here looking for that missing book."

"So, I guess reconstruction of the events is impossible."

"Not entirely," Mark said, as Tyler joined him at the window frame that once held the floor-to-ceiling glass, but now was replaced with a single strip of yellow police tape stretched across the opening. "Did you know Sammy Moore?"

"No, who's that?"

"That was one of Stephen's guards. It was his body we found this morning right over there. He took a bullet in the back of his head. Which is understandable; why the hell would he suspect Claire of anything? She was Stephen's squeeze. She'd been up here almost every night. Sammy didn't have a chance. As soon as he turned his back, she popped him."

"So, how do you think the rest of it played out?" said the thin man and lit another smoke.

"As it turns out, Stephen had the books and was taking them to New York. The cover story worked pretty well. Everybody thought they were locked up in the bank. Well, everybody except Claire. So, she came up here, killed Sammy, and forced Stephen to hand them over." After contemplating the scenario, Burnwell walked across the room to a small end table next to a bloody black leather wing-backed chair facing the picture window.

"It ended with Truman sitting here and Claire there where you are. She had the books and must have been about to shoot, when something happened. Maybe Sammy moved, maybe the phone rang. Whatever it was, it was just enough of a distraction for Stephen to grab his pistol from the table drawer and get off a round. They must have fired simultaneously, amazingly each hit center mass. The punch from the bullet knocked her out the window."

"What kind of weapon did Stephen have?"

"Thirty eight Chief Special. We found it just there by his feet. Fingerprints on the gun match his."

"What about the gun Claire used?"

"No luck there, Tyler. The weapon was covered with snow."

"How did Claire know Stephen had the books?"

"Good question," said Mark. He walked over to a framed piece of Schlock Art leaning against the wall and turned it over. "She bugged the place as well as his phone. We found a microphone on the back of this."

"Who the hell was this woman, Mark?"

"Far more than some simple second rate lawyer. When we went to her house, it was like stepping into a James Bond movie. There were stacks of money from six countries, bugging equipment, fake passports, some kind of weird looking two-way radio, and my favorite, a disguise kit. She was a cold blooded contract killer."

"Claire?" Longvue's face twisted in disbelief when the word fell from his lips. "Do you have any idea who she worked for?"

"No. Nothing at her place tied her to anyone. She was good."

"Well, not that good, fat boy," Tyler said, turning his attention back out the window and looking at where Anjou's body had landed. He took the final pull from his Marlboro, put it out on the window frame, and flicked the butt out the window. As he watched it fall to the ground, something occurred to him.

"Claire was hit one time in the chest with a .38 caliber bullet, so how..?" Suddenly the rail-thin detective became energized. He turned from the window and made his way quickly to the door.

"Come on, big fella, let's go to Claire's place."

"Why? We've already been over it and processed the evidence."

"Twenty bucks says something was missed."

"I'm just taking your money, Stickman, but you're on. What makes you think we overlooked something?"

"Trigonometry," said the determined Texan as he went out the door.

Stephen Huey

Borovo, UN Transitional Area

It appeared Burnwell was right. After an hour of rummaging in and around Claire's small Serbian home, Longvue had come up empty. Even the landlady's old black and white Springer spaniel had given up on the highly invigorated policeman. From a vantage point on the porch, the dog now rested his head on his paws and simply watched the two men standing outside the house.

"Just fork it over, Stickman. There's nothing more to be found."

"It appears you're right. You guys did a thorough job in here. I take it all the evidence is at HQ?"

"Yep," said Burnwell with his hand out.

Unhappily, Longvue dug into his pocket and retrieved some cash. He peeled off his debt and put it in the big man's waiting paw.

"Damn it. I was sure I was on to something."

"It's a pleasure to do business with you, son," cracked the tickled cop, counting his loot.

Taking in and exhaling a deep breath, Longvue looked at the lazy canine and lit a cigarette. In an off-handed manner he asked, "What did the landlady have to say when you questioned her?"

"We didn't question her."

"Why not?"

"First of all, it's highly unlikely that ancient woman had anything to do with Claire. And second, no one in our group spoke Serbian."

Snatching the money back, Tyler said, "But I do. Let's go."

As the two walked toward the owner's home, the aged Spaniel jumped up and barked viciously. Unfortunately for Longvue, this was the only excitement to be found after questioning the old Serbian landlady.

In short, he discovered that the owner had neither seen nor heard anything untoward concerning Claire the entire time she'd lived there. In fact, it was rare for her tenant to be around since she spent so much time away and with Stephen. The old woman said she let the dog out last night around midnight and saw Claire, or more precisely, she saw her car come into the drive. When the dog came back, the landlady locked the doors, turned out the lights, and went to bed.

Mark took back his $20.

chapter

FIFTEEN

Dubrovnik, Croatia

Winter took nothing from the Old City. Surrounded by the Adriatic on three sides, the mixture of bright and faded orange tile roofs topping centuries of sun-bleached gray and white stone framed the ancient seaport in magnificent splendor. But on his walk along the Frana Sopila to the Hotel Argentina, Tyler paid little attention to the sights. Even when he stopped along the way, lit a smoke, and looked out upon the tethered boats gently rocking in the medieval harbor, he didn't see a thing. He was too deep in his own world.

Stephen Huey

More than two weeks had passed since the harrowing episode of "the books" had reached its climax. And for a minute, the Texan pondered the extraordinary chain of recent events; the relentless pursuit by an Irish killer, the rapacious duplicity of a trusted colleague, the bizarre denouement of a secret assassin, and the merciless trail of carnage left in its wake. Consideration of the human toll had pushed through in Tyler's mind, and it was staggering. But the backward glance, as powerful as it was, only lasted for a short time because his well-developed defense mechanism kicked in.

Survival in a war zone meant mental gymnastics; therefore, events had to be compartmentalized. One learned to stay in the present, in the moment. To do otherwise, with the future or the past, meant frustrating uncertainty with the former and crushing despair from the latter. It wasn't easy, but it was required.

Maybe it was altogether appropriate that one of "the books" was thought lost forever in the Drava River, Longvue surmised. Then, as quickly as the thoughts had appeared, they were pushed back to their dark corners and replaced with the task at hand. He turned his face to the east and continued toward the Argentina.

Entering the hotel lobby precisely at 11:07, Longvue spotted his Russian interlocutor having coffee. Through the smoke of his constant cigarette, Nikita Zavisha greeted him with his trademark enigmatic smile.

"Comrade, come," Zavisha said and waved him over.

Seated in an alcove away from the main area, there was a large window to Nikita's back offering a grand view of the Adriatic. Longvue arrived at the chair opposite his friend and studied him. There were long vulgar scratches on both sides of the Russian's face near the eyes.

Looks like his extracurricular activity was a little rough, thought Tyler.

"Coffee?"

"Yes, black."

"Of course," said Nikita as he poured from the warm Bodum, while keeping his eyes on his American chum. "Your letter was of some note. And without question, you believe what you wrote?"

"Would have been foolish of me to ask you here if I didn't," the Texan said as he took off his jacket and sat. "Look, I know you prefer to flit around like a June-bug before getting down to business, but we don't have that kind of time. It's a straightforward deal, just like I said in my note. I know how to work the code, and I know you have the books, so let's agree to a split of 50/50 and move on this thing."

"As easy as that, my friend?"

"Yeah, it is actually," proffered Longvue, lighting a Marlboro. "I know, given enough time, you'll break the code. But you're not going to have that kind of time. If we don't reach an agreement, the letter I sent you will also be sent to UN HQ, the Croatian and Serbian governments, the US Embassy, the Russian Embassy, and anyone else I can think of. Oh, and killing me isn't a good option either. If I'm not back in Zagreb by midnight, those letters will be on their way."

This was hardball, and it came fast; something unexpected from his "comrade." It caught the old KGB officer off balance, but only for a bit. Zavisha didn't rise to the top levels of the Soviet machine because he played nice; for him, this was a return to the old days. As he sat back, the former spook took stock, then verbally weighed his options.

"I only have to say your words are the lie. I don't see your threat as being of any consequence."

"Sure you can, Nikita. And it'll probably work for a little while. But there will be that nasty investigation; who knows what they might find? And you'll be watched, by everybody, which makes hiding new-found wealth tough."

"Why would anyone believe your letter?" chided the Muscovite. "You erroneously accused me of stealing the books but you failed to offer any proof."

"The letter I sent you was, well, Nikita, let's call it the *Reader's Digest* version. I'll be sending our friends a full account detailing everything you did."

Longvue had hit the quick and he hammered it. He knew he had found his mark because Zavisha shifted in his chair a few times. And when he spoke, the Russian's tone had clearly switched from congenial and controlling to defensive and uncomfortable.

"And what is this everything you speak of?"

"I simply explain how you killed Claire, the body guard, and Stephen. Then you took the books and made it look as if Anjou had done it all. That about covers it, I think."

"I don't believe you. This is a fantasy, and you're the fool," stormed Zavisha getting up to leave.

"I admit, it's a singular chain of events but I've linked them all together carefully. Your story starts with trigonometry and ends with a bad disguise. But you walk out that door and it will no longer be a secret."

Nikita hesitated. He looked hard at his blackmailer. The treasure and the books had affected everything and everyone. It seemed, once touched, the desire for the vast wealth was an uncontrollable urge.

Tyler knew the big Russian was in a corner and needed to find out two things rather quickly; what it was Tyler actually knew about the incident and what the Russian was going to do about the clever thin man. Stalling for time, he slapped his gloves down on the table, tossed his long black cashmere overcoat across the back of the chair, and took a seat. Nikita lit another cigarette off the ember of the previous and locked his cold, dead, black eyes on the greedy cop from Houston.

"I think I have all the details," remarked Longvue as he sat back with his coffee. "But if I miss anything, feel free to jump in."

His listener sat stoic.

"You had been eavesdropping on Stephen for a long time. His phone, his office, his home; they were all bugged, so there wasn't much you didn't hear. And to be fair, I think you were just doing your job, but then the books came along, and everyone's outlook changed."

Tyler turned his gaze to the window and stared out into the distance at the blurred horizon of gray and blue. Where one stopped and the other started was hard to tell; *all fitting*, Longvue thought. Returning to his companion, he continued his narrative.

"Your change came about on the night you told us you were going to a conference in Paris. That was when

Stephen Huey

you had learned Stephen was taking "the books" to New York the next morning. More than a billion dollars, right there at your fingertips, was about to slip away; and you couldn't let that happen. You had the means, you had the motive, and now you had to act fast.

"Unfortunately, I think Claire was an afterthought. When you learned she had decided to forgo her trip to Paris and accompany Stephen to New York, she presented a useful and convenient fall guy. So, after midnight, you put your plan into action.

"First, you went over to Claire's house and planted all that spy paraphernalia; bugging equipment, passports, money. It was a first-class job. When her place was inspected the next day, everyone was fooled. From all appearances, she looked like a real operator, and that would have been the end of the investigation but for one thing.

"I learned no one had talked to the old Serbian landlady because none of the investigators spoke Serbo/Croat. So, I took it upon myself and, after three separate interviews, the old girl told me something peculiar. Seems on the night of Claire's death, the landlady saw Anjou's car pull into the drive well after midnight. She was certain of this because she was letting her dog out at the time, and she assumed it was Claire because she recognized the vehicle and the dog didn't bark."

"What does that prove? This dog that doesn't bark in the night?" questioned Nikita, unimpressed.

"It proves the dog knew the person. Like I said, I had to talk to the owner three times. Finally, after a little money changed hands, she told me that you used to live in the house, prior to Claire. Seems you rented the place

172

for about six months and the dog knew you well. Consequently, since the old woman saw the car, but didn't see Claire per se, and since you two drive the same kind of white Peugeot ... "

"And so do fifty other people in the mission. That's nothing," scoffed Nikita.

"By itself, yes, but not when the dog is considered. The landlady told me her hound is protective, especially at night. With the animal being friendly, you were able to go about your work. And when you finished, you simply rolled the little white car out of the drive and down the street. Once out of earshot of the old lady, you started it and continued on with your plan. Which gets me to the heart of the matter; the penthouse at the Hotel Osijek.

"To say the crime scene was a wreck is charitable. The only credible work accomplished was the initial investigation and the excellent attention to detail by a young Croatian beat cop, which I'll get to later."

Longvue stood and looked out over the cold Adriatic. His accused remained quiet, but his darting eyes showed his curiosity was piqued.

"Up in the penthouse I kept looking at where Claire's dead body had landed and its relation to the building. Finally, it occurred to me," the lean detective mused, "the answer was in trigonometry."

Turning back to his counterpart, Longvue continued. "One round from a .38 caliber pistol, fired from across the room, wouldn't have the punch to knock Claire that far away from the high-rise; the distances were all wrong. Something, or someone, had thrown her out of the penthouse with a great deal of force. Mulling it over, the only plausible explanation was that there was a fourth person in the room; the killer. Looking at it from that angle, the entire sequence of events played out for me as if I had been present.

"Clearly, it was someone they all knew, such as you, because, other than the broken window, there was no sign of struggle. With the element of surprise on your side, the sequence of events moved along efficiently.

"First, you capped Sammy Moore from close range in the back of the head. Then, you quickly shot Stephen, who was sitting stunned, I'm sure. Now came the tricky part.

"To fix the blame on Anjou, you needed two things; a bullet from Stephen's .38 in her, and her fingerprints on the weapon that you were using. So, you clocked Anjou with a pistol whip and put her out cold. From there it was simple. You walked over to the table where you knew Stephen kept his pistol, took it from the drawer, and turned to finish the job. But that's when your plans went south.

"Claire Anjou didn't stay down and she didn't run. She attacked you," said Longvue as he dragged his fingers alongside his face. The Russian neither looked at him nor showed any emotion.

"It's obvious she came up from behind. The wounds are deep near your cheek, then taper off as the marks come toward your ears. I'm thinking she both startled and angered you. It was with a lot of force that you slung her off. Now, the hotel windows aren't safety glass; that's a hard commodity to come by in a war zone and way too expensive. Therefore, when Claire hit it with momentum, she popped through easily. But this surprise didn't knock you out of the game; in fact, at that moment, your luck was making a remarkable comeback.

"To start, you had the presence of mind and the dead aim to put a bullet into her as she went out the window. Next, that side of the hotel faces the river, miles of open real estate, and there are no lights. Then, *the books* must have been in Stephen's attaché case because the hotel safe appeared undisturbed. Finally, being careful not to expose yourself to any possible witnesses below, you tossed one of the books and your weapon out the window behind her. Having the other book safely in your hands, the one that hadn't been copied, the only thing left to do was leave.

"Now, remember the beat cop I told you about? Around 2:00 that morning, he was called over to the Hotel Osijek to roust a collection of vagrants who had piled up in the lobby. They were drunk, and management wanted them off the property. It was a routine matter. These guys weren't bad; they were just bums coming in from the cold, and the cop knew all of them, except one.

"When the officer arrived, most of the street crew had already vacated. He grabbed the last two stragglers and was on the way out when the stairwell door to the lobby opened and out shuffled this peculiar looking fella with a backpack. The policeman was certain he hadn't seen him before because this guy looked rough. The man had a terrible stoop, long greasy gray and black hair, a right arm that appeared useless, and a scar running from his forehead to his chin, like a bullet had creased his face. You used the disguise to get upstairs. Took it off, did the job, then put it back on to escape."

Nikita snapped his eyes on those of his prosecutor.

"Just one problem; that was the same disguise you used at the Hollywood Bar," Tyler said, finishing his coffee. "Should have tried something new."

Perhaps two or three minutes went by without a word being spoken. Then, mechanically, the one-time Russian spy raised his big hands and slowly clapped.

"An excellent performance, and you can prove nothing."

"I'll take my chances. But proving this case in court is a long way down the road. The more immediate effect is what gives me leverage. When the word gets out, and it will, your life is going to be a living hell. A lot of *very persuasive* people want that money. I don't know if you've thought about your family, but I'm sure they will. And believe me, if they can't find you, well, someone else close to you will have to pay."

As was his nature, something Longvue had counted on, Nikita Zavisha reached a decision immediately. He got up from his chair and prepared to leave. "If you want that we do business, you'll come with me," he said and, without waiting for an answer, headed to the door. Seeing he had hit his mark, Longvue grabbed his things and obliged.

It was a short, swift, and quiet walk from the Argentina back to the Old City. Since the war, tourism had dropped to nothing. Where once the streets teemed with people year-round, now the only visitors were folks from the United Nation's mission and some adventurous German bargain hunters. The two entered the ancient stone fortress from the east side and had just passed Saint Luke's Church when Zavisha turned on his would-be partner. With his strong left forearm planted firmly under

Longvue's chin, Nikita pushed his target against the high wall. In his right hand there appeared a 9mm Beretta, which he pressed hard into Tyler's ribs.

"You think me stupid?"

"No, Nikita, very much the opposite," replied the Texan coolly. "You're doing exactly what I'd do. I'm not wired. Go ahead and check me."

With that, the highly suspicious Muscovite performed a thorough inspection. He checked every bit of Longvue's frame and everything on it; his knit cap, pockets, jacket, socks, and his shoes. Nikita even dismantled Tyler's Zippo lighter and emptied out his pack of Marlboros. But there were no bugs; the thin man was clean.

"Jesus, Nikita, I need a cigarette."

With that, his new Russian partner extended the flame from his lighter along with a decided change in his demeanor.

"You'll forgive me, Tyler. Trust but verify, you remember your president."

"Yeah, but he was talking about checking for nukes, not a colonoscopy," said Longvue, buttoning his coat and putting on his cap. "So, where do we go from here?"

Suddenly, the sound of several voices speaking different brands of loud English came from around the corner. A few moments later, there appeared seven slightly inebriated United Nations police monitors headed right for them. It was just another group of UN cops on holiday, some from New York and others from Ireland, taking advantage of the cheap prices in the coastal city. One in the group recognized Tyler and made a beeline for him.

"Howdy, Tex," bellowed Patrick, a more sober member of the crowd. "What the hell are you doing out here? I thought you were in Zagreb."

"I was," returned Longvue as his group of police buddies surrounded him. Because of close quarters in the walkway, Zavisha was edged out of the group.

"Let me introduce one of my colleagues, guys. This is Nikita Zavisha, one of UNTAES's top lawyers."

Putting his hand on Nikita's shoulder, Pat looked at him eye-to-eye. "Oh, yeah. I've seen him around. But we've never met." Extending his hand, he continued, "Good to finally do so. Hey, you guys want to join us for lunch?"

"We'll be leaving for Zagreb soon, sorry we can not," Nikita replied, turning his attention back to Tyler.

"Suit yourself. It's not often I pay."

"That's wrong. You never pay."

"Funny guy, Stickman. See ya."

When the good comrades were out of sight, Longvue dropped his smile and turned back to his new partner. "Like I said, where do we go from here?"

Upon entering the ancient walled city of Dubrovnik, the two confederates stepped along the eleventh century main street, Stardun. Taking a seat at one of the many empty open-air coffee shops along the 900-year-old thoroughfare of highly polished stone, their business began.

Instantly, a waiter appeared. Longvue tossed his pack of smokes onto the table and ordered a round of coffee and cognac.

"I'm not convinced we should share by halves."

"Why not?"

"Tyler, I've taken the greater risk. You have knowledge, yes, but I was the beast."

"You know what? I'm not going to argue. We're talking about something neither of us fully understands. Kazuko said there was probably more than a billion dollars tied up in those books. It's broken down equally into ten accounts. Give me four and you can have the others."

"I give you two."

"Damn, you'd think we're haggling over the price of a fish. This is a billion dollars. I've never seen a billion of anything." Tyler pulled out a fresh smoke and lit it. He looked up from his lighter and snapped shut the flame, "I'll take three."

"It's done. My friend you surprise me. I didn't think you so, pragmatic."

"Neither did I," replied Longvue. "Man, you just gave me $300 million. Let me savor it a bit. There will never, ever, be another time such as this. The instant we both took full control of our own destiny. All of our lives we've worked for the Machine. Now, it works for us."

"Yes, I think you have it right."

"Well, it looks like a question of mechanics from this point. You give me my accounts and I'll give you the formula. We can leave tonight and go to the location ... "

"Why should we leave?"

The thin man turned an astonished visage toward his companion. "You have the books with you?"

"Where else would they be?" the old KGB officer said and tapped the breast pocket of his coat. "No one knows about this but us."

Stephen Huey

Their waiter arrived and set the round in front of them. Taking his drink Zavisha raised it. "Nostro no, no, I think this is to us."

Tyler seconded the toast, both men drained their shots, and the slim Texan signaled for another round. At that point, the enormity of the episode knocked the two newly minted multimillionaires into silence. But it was only for a moment before surrealism latched on and both broke into loud long laughter.

"Now, to the work." Producing "the books" from his pocket, Nikita set them on the table. Neither of the wide-eyed partners could say a word; nothing else mattered. They had survived the bloody contest, they had outwitted all their opponents, and the spoils were theirs, alone. Their focus, future, their world was all right there in two small volumes simply waiting to unfold into a life larger than their dreams.

"I'll take those," punched the solid voice of Mark Burnwell while his big left hand grasped the two books. The crashing power of Nikita's arms flipped the table as he tried to stop him. But three UN policemen, part of the group from earlier, swiftly followed Burnwell from inside the restaurant and put a quick end to the desperate Russian's actions.

"I didn't know how much longer I could keep this up," groused Longvue, wiping his jacket clean of the water and coffee, which had sprayed him when the table turned over. "What took you so long?"

"Look, Stickman, it's not like there's a big crowd of people we can hide in. Coming in the back way takes some time."

"Did you get everything?"

"Loud and clear."

Tyler lit a fresh cigarette, took a seat, and watched while a couple of UNTAES police officers cuffed and searched Zavisha. Finishing with their catch, they brought him to his feet and were about to lead him away.

"You're making terrible mistake. I'll make you pay."

"That's the best you have? Man, I miss the old days," quipped Burnwell. "Nikita, threaten me like it's 1975, bang your shoe on the table, get some fire. Not, 'I will make you pay;' that's just, just, corny."

Before leading him away, Tyler picked up the pack of Marlboros that had been knocked off the table and shook out a small listening device. "Nikita there's just one last thing." Holding up the tiny object, which was about the size of a Chiclet, he continued. "This gadget recorded everything we said. Oh, you're not going crazy. It wasn't there when you searched me earlier. I had a prearranged signal with the boys here. If I was wearing my cap when they came up on us, they knew to slip me the pack of cigarettes. Remember when Pat introduced himself? That was the moment."

To this, the captured Muscovite said nothing. With hands secured to his back, it was he who turned and made the first step away with a police escort on each side.

"Do you know how lucky you are?" started Burnwell, in a voice impressed and annoyed with his skinny friend. "We had you two under observation the entire time, so there wasn't a chance that he was going to get away. But what if Nikita hadn't checked you over when the guys first showed up? They couldn't keep circling and bumping into

Stephen Huey

you. He would have gotten suspicious. What would you have done then?"

"Guess I would have kept the $300 million he offered me and thought of something else."

"Well, here's your reward," Mark said and pitched a wadded $20 bill to Longvue. "Think about that." With a grin, the big man turned and walked away to join the others. "Glad you're on our side, Stickman, but honest to God I don't know how you do it."

"I'm just a cop. Why do I have to keep reminding everyone?"

"You really don't get it?" Burnwell replied without turning back to his partner. "Yeah, you're just a cop, but that's not an answer, it's a question."

Watching the sun disappear in winter's gray lugubrious sky, an equally melancholy Longvue reached over to refill his empty Rakia glass. He was the only person on the Hotel Argentina's patio restaurant, and in his mood that was exactly the way he wanted it.

"Why don't you slow down on those things?"

Turning quickly, Tyler surprisingly found himself face-to-face with Kazuko.

"When did you leave Zagreb?"

"I caught the bus right after you called. I didn't want to wait."

Considering the situation, that was an extremely dangerous move, and they both knew it. But those concerns vanished as one kiss led to another.

"Are you all right, Tyler?"

"Yeah, I'm fine. It was a hell of a day, though. Mark and the boys were perfect. It all went off without a hitch. I'm still surprised Margaret went along with the whole thing."

"She loved Stephen. Doesn't surprise me in the least," said Nakamura, taking a seat while Tyler poured her a glass. "And we both know what's going to happen to Zavisha."

"Yeah, nothing," grumbled Longvue. "That Russian son-of-a-bitch killed three good people and he's going to walk away because of diplomatic immunity. And there's not a damn thing we can do about it."

"Perhaps."

"What does that mean?" he asked.

"He may never be brought to court, but neither will he have the riches that he so desperately wanted."

"That's poetic, I guess, but practically speaking he's not going to suffer one bit," remarked the soured Texan.

"As far as he knows."

"Why are you talking in riddles?"

"Because, Stickman, I'm pretty good at solving them. Take solace in the fact that neither Nikita Zavisha, nor anyone else in the world for that matter, will ever know what happened to every single dime locked up in those books. Some of that money is gone and it will never be discovered missing."

Turning to her, the thin man squinted, "What are you driving at?"

"Remember when we were in the bus returning to Osijek from Zagreb? You were up front with the Russian soldier and I was in the back, 'working on the books'," she said with emphasis. "What do you think I was doing?"

END